BEFORE TIMES

3 VALKYRIE BESTIARY PREQUELS

KIM MCDOUGALL

Published by Wrongtree Press.
Editing by Elaine Jackson.
Cover art by Pamela Francescut.
Cover Design by Genevieve Chatel.

Version 1

Paperback ISBN: 978-1-990570-05-6

FICTION / Fantasy / Urban
FICTION / Fantasy / Paranormal

About This Book

Before Times is a collection of three Valkyrie Bestiary prequel tales.

The Last Door to Underhill: In the last hours of the Flood Wars, a fae princess makes the ultimate sacrifice to save the human world. This tale takes place about 50 years before the events of *Dragons Don't Eat Meat.*

The Girl Who Cried Banshee: Kyra Greene is a pest controller, not an exterminator. She has to be clear about that when the pests can be anything from pixies to dragons. But when her fledgling business teeters on the brink of bankruptcy, Kyra takes on a job that blurs those lines. This tale takes place about 10 years before the events of *Dragons Don't Eat Meat.*

Three Half Goats Gruff: Kyra Greene, pest controller of fantastic beasts, takes on a rock troll and meets the man who will haunt her dreams for the next three-hundred and twenty-one nights. Come sing around the campfire with satyrs and discover how Kyra found one little lost cephalopod. This tale takes place about 1 year before the events of *Dragons Don't Eat Meat.*

BOOKS BY KIM MCDOUGALL

The Hidden Coven Series:
Inborn Magic
Soothed by Magic
Trigger Magic
Bellwether Magic
Gone Magic

Valkyrie Bestiary Series
Dragons Don't Eat Meat
Dervishes Don't Dance
Hell Hounds Don't Heel
Grimalkins Don't Purr
Kelpies Don't Fly
The Girl Who Cried Banshee (Novella)
Three Half Goats Gruff (Novelette)
The Last Door to Underhill (Novelette)

Writing as Eliza Crowe

The Shifted Dreams Series:
Pick Your Monster
Lost Rogues

Contents

For Griffin.

THE LAST DOOR TO UNDERHILL

Saguaro Door

June 2027

I STOOD BETWEEN worlds—one foot planted firmly in Underhill, the other reluctant to leave Arizona. Behind me, the burning suburbs of Tucson lit the night like constellations. Smoke blurred out the real stars. But it was the silence that was terrifying. The bombs had stopped falling, and the sirens had run out of fuel. The few ragged humans and fae who'd survived the journey from Phoenix filed through the portal to collapse on wildflower-pocked hills, too exhausted to marvel at the splendor of the fae world. On their arrival, a swarm of bumble sprites erupted from the flowers, *tsking* and vibrating in annoyance. Elves, imps and goblins wearing the king's deep burgundy rushed to bring water and medical supplies to the refugees.

When did I last taste water? I couldn't remember. Hours. Days. But I wouldn't stand down until the last of our group crossed through the gate. I gazed into the desert, willing more refugees to sneak from the shadows of the great saguaros. The short nights of early summer had worked in our favor. The demon couldn't hunt under the Terran sun. Sunrise was the only reason we'd escaped that morning. But the long day was done now. He'd be coming for us.

I shivered, more from exhaustion than the brisk wind blowing off the desert.

"Soldier!" a voice barked from behind me. "Move away from the gate!"

My helmet—stolen from a dead fae somewhere outside Chandler—was too big, and it fell over my eyes. I tipped back the brim, and light from the bright but sunless Underhill sky struck my face.

The sergeant dropped to his knees.

"Princess Leighna! I did not see you." Then he stumbled over that insult. To unsee a fae was the greatest punishment, akin to banishment. "I mean…I did not recognize you."

"It's all right, Sergeant." My voice rasped from a dry throat. "My own mother wouldn't recognize me today."

My attire was a far cry from the elegance of the Winter Court. I wore a mishmash of clothing taken from safe houses as we'd run across a burning continent, and these were torn and bloody. Soot and dirt caked every bit of exposed skin. Under the dented helmet, my silver hair had long ago matted so badly that I'd lopped it off with a hunting blade. But my magic still sang like a princess—I couldn't disguise that—and the soldier had enough keening to sense it.

For weeks, I'd been berating, urging, and cajoling humans and fae toward Saguaro Door and the safety of Underhill. Trying to convince them to run when bombs were falling wasn't easy. Spurring them to make the long trek into the desert was harder.

I sagged against the stone pillar that marked the doorway. "How many refugees came through in the last week?"

"Not enough." The sergeant handed me a canteen. I drank deeply as he gave his report. "A thousand, maybe 0. And more than half were human."

So few. Fear and despair fought for dominion in my stomach. Too many fae had been lost in the Terran war already. And the humans? I shuddered. In another month, the few hundred humans who'd made it to Underhill might be the last of their race.

"I must get word to my father." I stepped both feet onto my home soil for the first time in ten years. "This door will be terminated."

"But, my lady!" The sergeant protested. "We cannot close it! By King's command."

I grabbed him by the shoulder. "There is no more time. Horak follows us." He blanched. Speaking a demon's true name aloud gave him power to manifest, but I didn't worry about that now. It was too late. Horak already had our scent.

The demon spent the spring, burning, raping and killing his way through the state of Arizona. It had been pure bad luck that he caught up to us in Phoenix. But fae magic was the nectar of demons. He wouldn't let us go. And by now, he could smell the gate to Underhill and all that delicious fae magic beyond it.

"How long?" asked the sergeant.

I glanced at the night sky and rubbed my gritty eyes. How long until the demon found us? Two hours? Less? We'd left him on the outskirts of Tucson at first light when he'd slunk into a sewer to wait out the sun. I'd run my little band of stragglers all day, though they had nothing left to give. We hiked into the mountains, pushing the slowest to keep up, stopping to rest when they couldn't. Horak's powers were limited on Terra, but he could fly. In a few hours, he'd cover the twenty miles we'd labored all day to cross.

"He'll be an hour behind," I said. "No more."

A crowd of soldiers and refugees had gathered around us. I turned to the worn out, terrified faces. They wanted guidance, and I had none left to give. Instead, I pushed through them, heading for the gatehouse.

"Where's the gatekeeper?"

"Here, my lady." An aging dwarf scurried forward, nearly tripping over the long brown sackcloth he wore like a monk's habit.

"Gander!" The sight of my old arcane arts teacher filled me with renewed hope.

His eyes raked me up and down and he frowned. I worried he might do something stupid like bow.

"Princess, you look like shite."

"And you smell like the bottom of an ale pot."

He glared, and then his mustache twitched. "Lass, I've missed you."

I crouched, and the old dwarf hugged me.

"Now, what's this talk about closing the door? It's unstable, but I'm sorting that." He held up an antique scroll.

I shook my head. "Too late for that. Horak's coming."

Gander's shaggy brows arched. Then he turned to the sergeant.

"Get everyone away from the door!"

"You heard 'im!" the sergeant shouted. "Move out!"

Grumbling groans rose from the refugees, but they picked up their tired bodies and followed the soldiers, heading deeper into the stark beauty of Underhill.

"Make sure they have housing," I said. "And no one goes hungry. By order of the king." The sergeant nodded. I didn't have the authority to make demands in my father's name, but he didn't argue.

Gander returned carrying a long, curved blade. The sword's magic sang to me, an old song full of lament and lost chances. My fingers ached to grip it.

"None of that." Gander yanked the blade out of my reach. "Tis a potent thing, I know, but you need years of practice to wield it without getting lost in its lure."

I held my hands rigid at my side. I wanted that blade. "What's it for?"

"To cut the ties binding the door to this world. But lass, are you sure of this? We could power down the generators, close the gate until the danger passes."

I shook my head. "Horak can break through any crack in the veil. Only a complete seal will stop him. Destroy it. And hurry!"

"It will be done." Gander nodded but the edges of his voice were ragged. This door and eight others that dotted Underhill were his life's work. No one knew more about the doors than Gander. Destroying one was like killing his child.

He gripped the blade and headed toward the jumble of gears and wires that made up the gate's engine.

A horse leapt through the door. It was lathered and puffing, and a girl tumbled from the saddle.

"Please! We need help!" Her words were muddled with panic. Something about another group of refugees.

"Who sent you?" I asked when she sucked in a breath.

"Timberfoot Greenleaf. He asks for horses to carry the children. They slow the group. That…that thing is chasing us!" Great gobs of tears choked her. I could get little more information. Only that this Timberfoot was an hour's ride south.

I conferred with the sergeant. "How many soldiers can you send?"

He scratched his chin. "Six. No more."

"Do it."

WHEN MAGIC RETURNED to Terra, thousands of fae emigrated, drawn to the exciting and excitable humans. Then the humans did what they do best. They weaponized it. The first magic bombs decimated entire cities. They called the ensuing disaster the Flood Wars because of the magical deluge that changed the landscape forever, swelling ley-lines and oceans, reclaiming cities with wild forests, and making it possible for exiled magical beings of all kinds to return to the planet.

The Duannae of Underhill who'd made a home on Terra hunkered down. We were determined to wait out the madness. When it became clear that the humans were on a path of self-annihilation, some fae returned to Underhill, but more stayed on Terra, hoping to claim it as our own when the ashes settled.

Then the humans learned to open gates to other realms and let a demon into their world. Horak could not open a door in the veil alone. He needed the cooperation of someone on the other side—a foolish human with a thirst for power to give him a toehold on Terra. That arrogant sorcerer who thought he could control forces from a demon world—was Horak's first victim. After that, Horak had free rein to terrorize, rape, and murder. And if the demon found one of the hidden doors to Underhill, he would bring that trifecta of horror to fae country.

Only the fae knew where to find the doors between Terra and Underhill. The fae and a few lucky humans who stumbled on them by accident. I'd been running toward Saguaro Door for weeks, gathering refugees along the way. For the first time in Underhill's history, the Duannae welcomed humans with open arms. We were all brothers and sisters in this battle. At least I hoped that's how the King and his Council would see it.

Now, as I waited for the last refugees, I wondered. Maybe I shouldn't have run for Saguaro door when I knew Horak hunted us. Maybe I should have led him away from Underhill. But the selfishly terrified part of me screamed to go home. The less selfish side knew that Underhill was the only haven for these poor people who had nowhere else to go.

And now that I was home, Saguaro Door would be sacrificed. I would have to close it before Horak found his way to the magic-rich land of my ancestors.

I stared into the dark Arizona desert full of deceptive shadows and willed Timberfoot Greenleaf to hurry. Every second we delayed put my people in danger. If Horak came first, I'd have no choice but to close the door and leave Timberfoot and his refugees to their fate.

To the west, a city-center tower collapsed, sending smoke and ash spiraling into the sky. It was terrifying to watch, but also mesmerizing and beautiful. Terra was so…so much. It had extremes that the Duannae could never imagine. A scorching sun. Flooding rains. Deserts, swamps and icecaps. Darkness and light. My fae home had none of these. Underhill was lovely and constant, a never-ending sweet summer day, a boundless blue sky without even the orb of a sun to blind you. Which was why the fae had flocked to Terra as soon as the ley-lines swelled. We craved the diversions and many-hued passions of the humans.

I paced the cooling desert. Where was this Timberfoot? He'd better bring an army, or we didn't stand a chance. The king's guard held the Underhill side of the portal, but how long could we hold out? Waiting for Timberfoot might save a few dozen lives. How many more would die if Horak crossed through the door? The demon craved magic, and his cravings consumed him. He would drink Underhill dry, leaving it a barren husk before moving onto the next world.

We had to stop him here. Perhaps Terra was already lost, but I wouldn't lose Underhill too.

"It's time," I said. We'd waited long enough. Too long. "Everyone back through the door."

"My lady, look!" The soldier to my left pointed. I sensed movement before I saw them. Six of the king's cavalry came first, each bearing a child on their saddle. We parted and they dashed through the door. The desert fell silent again.

Ten tense minutes later, the clouds shifted and moonlight exposed a long line of weary refugees trudging up the hill.

An explosion lit the sky, followed by an inhuman roar that filled every space in my head.

Horak was coming.

I clamped hands over my ears, but it didn't help. His scream shredded sanity, inciting pure terror. I fought through it and shouted, "This way!" But my words were thin armor against the demon's magic. A saguaro burst into flame beside the trail. The refugees scattered like bugs.

In the chaos, a stranger grabbed my hand. I jerked it away and looked up into startling green eyes. He towered over me—an oak tree come to life, with craggy features and a shag of red hair and beard. His magic tasted like spring leaves. A dryad.

Damn the gods! Just when I needed a general, they sent me a tree-hugger. "You're Timberfoot?"

He nodded. The wind picked up, rushing like a train across the mountain.

"That's the last of them," he yelled over the noise and pointed to the few desperate souls still struggling up the hill.

"Get them through the door! We're going to cut all ties to Terra!"

A spider troll mounted the rise and shimmied around a cactus, its claws clicking on bare rock. A needle of fear pierced my chest, and I stumbled backward. Taller than a dwarf, and with an eerily human face, the creature was covered in chitinous armor. It had two pairs of arms—one long and multi-jointed with large human hands, the other short with razor claws that clacked like mandibles when it sensed prey. A second troll followed the first and snapped its claws. A malicious grin spread across its face when it spied the unprotected humans and fae. These were Horak's minions, made by him, manifested from his dark magic. I'd been running from them for weeks. Always, they were only a step behind. We never slept, barely ate. We only ran and ran and ran until we had no other options.

Today, we had options.

Timberfoot scooped up a straggling woman and dashed for the shimmering door.

The hair on the back of my neck rose like cactus barbs. I turned. A figure stood on the mountain head, silhouetted against the faint light of the stars. Black horns protruded from his massive bald head. But for a gold cloth wrapped around his loins, he was naked. Flexing arms showed off ridges of muscle on his chest and shoulders. His skin was the color of dried blood, and he glowed from within. Even at this distance, I keened the dark miasma of death sloughing off him.

The demon spread his sinewy arms wide. His laugh rolled over me like thunder made of jagged ice. Wings burst from his back, and he launched into the sky, heading straight into the gate.

I dove through the door. Gander stood ready with his blade. Horak screamed and blasted the desert floor with his fire from his fingertips.

"Gander, now!"

Spiders swarmed the gate.

Gander slashed down. His blade screeched through the magical umbilical cord. The shimmering portal wavered. Its edges wrinkled and melted away like mist in the morning sun.

A dozen trolls skittered through the shrinking portal and dashed into the wilds of Underhill. Soldiers took off after them. The refugees panicked and ran in all directions. Then two black hands thrust through the doorway, grabbing blindly and caught one of the refugees as she ran by the gate. Long rust-colored fingernails tore a jagged strip of flesh from her face. The woman screamed. Blood spurted, soaking the demon as he stepped through to Underhill.

The door slammed shut behind him.

Gander cursed in the dwarven tongue beside me. I pulled him into the shadows.

The demon shook the wounded woman and roared, spraying her face with spittle. She fainted and hung like a limp dishrag in his hands. The demon exuded magic. It swirled about him in a cloud that seemed to suck in light.

Horak leaned down and breathed in the woman's scent. His black tongue ran a wet line from her throat to her forehead, and her skin shriveled where it touched. He was drinking her life magic! In a blink, he drained her and threw away the desiccated body. He stood taller now, suffused with his victim's energy. His wings spread like great black stains against the sky. And he roared, a sound that threatened to crack the ground under his feet.

Silence followed.

I tasted ash on my tongue, and the air had the rotten tang of brimstone. Humans and fae stared at the creature who stood grinning in the bright Underhill light. Then a child cried, breaking the shocked silence. People scattered. Soldiers ran forward. They pelted the demon with flaming arrows, shot him with human guns, tossed spells of undoing at him. None of those weapons could stop a demon.

"We ride for Winter City!" I yelled over the chaos in the yard.

"This way!" Gander pulled me toward the stables.

I looked back at the battle that was raging between the soldiers and Horak. Timberfoot was running after us with a crying child in his arms. I hoped he was worth it because I'd waited for him. And the delay had cost us everything. We would now need to close all the doors to Terra. Underhill was lost.

Duanna Door

With an escort from the Saguaro Garrison, I rode into Winter City. The garrison could mount a thousand men. The town that had grown up beside the door and its soldier barracks boasted another four thousand men and women. Five thousand souls, no matter how determined, couldn't stop a demon. But they were enough to slow him down, enough to let us get away and report to the king.

My heart ached for the death we left behind us.

We dismounted and gave our horses over to the South Gate guards. Gander agreed to accompany me to the palace. Timberfoot had nowhere else to go, so he followed. It seemed I had adopted a dryad honor guard somewhere along the way.

Winter City was the jewel of Underhill. The streets were clean and cobbled in pearlescent stone. At the city center, the palace—built from the same stone— rose like a glittering crown. Even from the gate, I spied its delicate white spires glowing against the blue sky.

News of the Saguaro battle hadn't reached here yet. The streets were busy, but the people moved with deliberation after a long day. No one was panicked. Vendors lined the road wending through town, hawking everything from fine silks, to birds in cages, to potions for beauty, love or revenge. A troll in a dusty apron displayed his three-tiered, rainbow frosted cakes with pride, swatting the pixies that buzzed around them, attracted by the sugar. A young dwarf polished shoes for coins on one corner. On another corner, a hag told fortunes from a colorful tent. Everywhere I looked, I saw the beautiful diversity that was Underhill. And magic. It was everywhere. Sparkling from the signs that lured people into shops. Floating on the scents of fresh bread. Glittering from the glamors worn by many fae. Magic imbued every cobblestone, every foundation. Winter City was forged with it.

It was the perfect beacon for a starving demon.

As we neared the palace, markets began to close. Several times, we had to stop and press ourselves against the walls as carts drawn by mules or reindeer vied for passage back to the gates, where they would return to their farms to stock up for tomorrow's market.

The city hadn't changed, but I had. The last time I walked these streets, I'd been dressed as a princess. People moved out of the way for me as I passed, bowing their heads in respect. Children often ran up to shyly hand me flowers.

Now, people still moved out of my way. Not in deference to my title, but to avoid brushing against my dirty, bloody, and torn clothes. And because of the hulking dryad that shadowed me.

A cart pulled up behind me, blocking Gander's path. I hated to leave the dwarf to battle the market traffic, but speaking to the king was most urgent.

"Go on!" He waved to me. "I'll catch up."

Timberfoot pushed the cart backward. The driver, a wiry imp with a squinty eye, let out a cry of outrage, until Timberfoot's shadow fell on him.

The dryad grinned. "Just want to help my friend." His teeth were very white against his ruddy complexion and the smile was more feral than pleasant. The imp shut up.

Timberfoot grabbed Gander by the collar and hauled him forward.

"I thank you—" Gander was cut off as Timberfoot swung him up to sit on his shoulders.

"How dare you! Put me down!" The dwarf sputtered and squirmed.

"Hold still." Timberfoot clamped his hands around the dwarf's ankles. "Do you want to get to the castle or not?"

"Aye." Gander's fuzzy brows lowered. "But 'tis most undignified."

I tried not to laugh, seeing my old tutor riding on Timberfoot's shoulders like a kid at a fair. "It's only a short distance. And no one will recognize us."

Gander gripped the dryad's hair and grumbled, "This big bull will be memorable enough."

"Moo," Timberfoot said with that untamed grin again.

We made it to Winter Palace as the light began to fade. Not wanting to offend anyone with our road dust, I led us toward the servants' entrance. It was guarded by two imps in the king's maroon.

"Move along!" One guard pointed his spear at us and waved it down the street.

"I must see the king. I have urgent business."

The imp looked me up and down. His nose wrinkled. My perfume wasn't too enticing after weeks on the road.

"The king won't see the likes of you." His lip lifted in a sneer. "If you have a petition, take it to the castellan's office. Tomorrow." He turned away.

I straightened my spine, took a deep breath, and infused my voice with the authority of my ancestors.

"I am Princess Leighna Icewolf. I demand to see my father, the king."

The soldier jerked to a stop like a puppet master had yanked on his strings. He turned and took my measure again.

"You're no princess."

"Do what she says, man." Gander squirmed down the mountainous dryad to stand before the soldier. "Get the castellan, if you need, but hurry. We have urgent business."

The guard recognized Gander, who had been a fixture at the palace since before I was born.

"Yes, sir!" He turned and dashed into the shadows of the castle, leaving us with the other guard, who watched us warily.

While we waited, I studied the palace. In the twilight hours, the faceless blue sky of Underhill dimmed to gray. The Winter Palace seemed lit from within, like icicles held near a flame. Delicate spires spiked into the sky, rising above slender towers. One of those towers had been my personal suite when I lived here. What had my parents done with it in my absence? Had they closed it up? Turned it into a fitness center or storage room?

Minutes went by. I slumped against the wall beside the servants' door. The guard eyed me like I might try to storm the castle. I glared back at him, and he stepped behind the half-shut door like a shield.

"Don't antagonize the wee laddy," Gander said. "He's just doing his job."

"I know." I ran a hand across my face. Both palm and cheek were gritty with road dust.

Now that we'd stopped, I noticed the dozens of aches in my body. My feet were damp and blistered. During that last fight, I'd taken a wound to the thigh and blood had dried to a crusty patch on my pants. My knee gave out and I sank to the ground.

Timberfoot handed me a canteen. I smiled and drank the tepid and slightly metallic-tasting water.

A laugh grated up from my chest.

"What's so funny?" Timberfoot asked.

"Just thinking that within those walls, hundreds of fancy-pants courtiers are sipping the finest wines and eating canapés. And here I am, wondering whose blood is on my jeans and drinking eau de canteen."

"I bet you're still prettier than those courtiers." Timberfoot winked.

"Really?" I held my dirty hands up with their raw, broken nails.

He straightened my helmet that always fell over my eyes.

"Really."

For the past day, as we rode hellbent for the palace, Timberfoot had been a looming presence beside me. For the first time, I really looked at him. He was taller than any fae I'd met, taller than my father who was known as the ice bear for his size. But while my father had the barrel chest of a grizzly, Timberfoot was fitter. Broad shoulders tapered to strong thighs. His hands were big and blunt, but oddly nimble in their movements. A red beard covered his chin and strawberry curls hung a little too low, hiding his gaze. And then the wind shifted, and I was gazing into his leaf-green eyes that glinted with mischief and untold secrets.

He took the canteen and spilled a bit of water over my hand, then rubbed my skin until it shone pink again.

"See? There *is* a princess under all that grime."

I felt my eyes heat up, threatening to spill tears down my face. It had been so long since anyone had thrown a kind word my way. So long that I'd been running from bombs, fires, and panicked humans. And the demon.

I squeezed his hand.

"Leighna!" A shrill voice had me scrambling to my feet.

"Mother?"

I ran and threw myself into her arms.

"Oh, my girl!" She hugged me despite the dirt I smeared across her fine gown. "What happened to you? I haven't had a word in nearly a year!" She held me at arm's length. "Why are you dressed like a beggar?"

"I've been running all day. For weeks, really. First from the bombs, then…" Some emotion clogged my throat—misplaced grief, overwhelming relief or a combination of the two.

"Oh, you poor child. We heard the Terrans had gone mad. I hoped you were well away from that mess."

There was no place on Terra that could escape the war.

Spectators gathered in the yard. Someone had recognized Queen Reneni. Whispered words were passed along, as the common folk wondered what brought her outside the servants' gate at dusk. I turned my back to them and pitched my voice low.

"Mother, the war is here. A demon came through Saguaro Door. We must take—"

"Shh!" She pulled me through the door and into the shadows of an alcove. "Do not speak of such things where others can hear."

"They will know soon enough! Horak is here in Underhill. We must act. I should speak to father." I tried to push past her, but mother was a formidable woman, despite her eight centuries. She stood almost six feet tall and wore her russet hair coiled around her head like a tower, adding to her height. She walked with the grace of an uprooted willow sapling. And she was dressed in a pale green silk gown with pearls sewn into it in vertical lines from bodice to hem. The skirt hugged her waist then flared like the head of a daffodil around her feet.

She wasn't dressed for a normal afternoon court. Damn the gods. I had no time for a formal ball.

"I need to see father in private."

"You will, but not dressed like that."

I forced myself not to fist my hands. Mother hadn't seen the things I'd seen in the past weeks. She hadn't pulled children from burning wreckage, only to find them already dead. She hadn't done head counts of the people she ran with, knowing at each stop a few more would be missing. She hadn't dodged aetheric bombs that leveled entire buildings. She hadn't faced a demon.

"I don't care who sees me." I waved a hand at my clothes. "This is too important."

"And that is why you will dress properly—"

"Mother! You don't understand!" I felt like a teenager again and I stamped my foot.

"No, you don't understand." She grabbed my arm and pulled me deeper into the palace. We were in the castellan's wing that housed his office, one for the housekeeper and other heads of household. She dragged me along the hall, past stunned maids and footmen, until we reached a small office. She pulled me inside and closed the door.

"Your father has not been well." Her voice was just above a whisper. "Seeing you dressed like a common foot soldier will not sit well with him. His mind is…delicate."

"What does that mean?" A new thorn of worry dug into my heart.

She laid her hands flat on the desk and breathed deeply. I wondered if her stays were too tight.

"It means that he's been having…episodes."

I raised one eyebrow at her in a way that I knew mirrored her own expression of frustration.

She sighed. "He's experiencing some dementia. The doctors aren't clear about the cause. We've been trying to keep his condition quiet. No one must know."

I paced in the small room. This was bad.

"Then who's in charge?"

She lifted her chin a small degree. "Me. And the council. For now."

"Where is Alvar?" If father was ill, my brother should be taking an active role on the Council.

"He's gone north to the Summer Garrison. He's a captain in the army now."

My little brother, a captain? I really had been gone too long. I still thought of him as a lazy and somewhat annoying youth. He'd only been seventy-five years old when I left, barely out of adolescence by Duannan standards.

"You must call him back. The army will have to gather here. It's the only chance we have of beating Horak."

"We'll take care of it." Mother folded me into her arms again. I never matched her height and my head rested under her chin. I breathed in the simple lavender perfume that she always wore. It was a scent that had soothed me since I was a child.

"Thank you."

She held me at arm's length and smiled. "Now go get cleaned up. Let your father see his beautiful girl not this mudlark."

By now, Gander would have already reported to the castellan. The Saguaro soldiers would tell their tales too. I was glad to give the reins of despair and worry over to someone else.

"You will speak to the Council?"

"I will." Mother kissed my filthy cheek.

"They'll want to hear from me." I sniffled. "I can give a full report. Gander too. He was there."

Mother nodded and pushed me toward the door.

"Everything will be all right. You'll see."

Because no one had been expecting me, my tower suite wasn't ready. I stood in a guest room overlooking the elegant roofs of parliament and the wealthier courtier homes. As the light faded, twinkling fairy lights came on all over the city. Winter City was spectacular, but its beauty was orchestrated. Each of the glassy spires represented a great house lost on the ancient world of Duanna. When the fae first came to Underhill, they built their cities with precision and forethought. They used magic to decorate them with an array of flowers, gems and works of art. But the city was almost too perfect.

Terran cities sprouted like weeds—sometimes graceful, sometimes inelegant—but wild and unpredictable in a way that Underhill could never be. Like the Underhill sky that never went completely dark. During the day, it was bright, faceless sheet of blue. At night, the brilliance grayed, but never went out.

There are reasons why people fear the dark, good reasons. The Terran sun is a big ball of magic that even scientists can only hope to fully understand. But it holds sway over many creatures, demons included. Under the eye-less sky of Underhill, Horak could rampage unchecked. He would decimate Underhill in a matter of months. Nothing that walked on two legs or four would be left alive. And then he'd move on to the next unsuspecting plane.

I had vowed not to let that happen—with or without sanction from the King's Council.

A parade of servants came through the room, bringing hot water, towels, fresh clothes, iced fruit juices.

When they finally left, I was alone with one elderly imp as an attendant.

"Were my companions seen to?" I asked.

"Yes, milady. The dwarf is back in his tower. The dryad has been given a guest room."

I was impatient and it felt indulgent to relax. So much was at stake, but

Mother was right. The Council would never take me seriously as I was.

I sighed and peeled off my clothes. My attendant took one look at the pile of bloody, filthy rags and dumped them in the fire.

I was too agitated to soak for long in the bath. The imp clucked and tsked.

"At least sit long enough for me to wash your hair!" She was an older imp, plump and strong. Mother had obviously chosen her for her no nonsense attitude.

"Fine." I sank back into the water. "But make it quick."

"No worries, milady. I'll have you ready in time for the ball."

"It's not the ball I'm worried about."

And then her strong fingers massaged my scalp, my neck and my shoulders. And for a brief interlude, I forgot the terror of the last weeks.

Half an hour later, I sat at the dressing table, staring at a face I barely recognized in the mirror. My hair was short and ragged. With its silver hue, I looked like a dandelion gone to seed. The imp pursed her lips and studied the problem, brushing it right, then left before giving up.

"You could glamor it. All ladies do it these days. A nice lattice braid might suit you."

"No glamor," I snapped. The imp puckered her lips in disapproval, and I softened my tone. "I won't be staying for the ball anyway."

I'd hoped that Mother would come by, if only to help me choose a gown. She never could resist dressing me like a doll. And I'd let her if it meant getting an update from the Council. But Mother didn't show up.

I chose an icy blue gown from a rainbow selection, not caring that it set off my eyes or flattered my silver hair. I only cared that it was the simplest design, long and plain except for the glittering white gemstones sewn into it like stars. If the night came to a fight, I could easily tear the skirt up one side to free my leg for a good kick.

I took one last glance at myself in the mirror and reached for my sword.

"You're not bringing that to the ball!" The maid looked aghast, like I had just pulled on the dead head of a wild boar as a mask.

I eyed the battered sheath. It really didn't fit my ensemble.

"Fine. But I'm bringing this." I tucked a small dagger into the garter around my thigh. "Now I'm ready for a party."

Someone had found Timberfoot court dress. He looked good. Really good. He'd shaved the beard, revealing a strong chin. His waistcoat was dark green, almost black, and downplayed his brawniness. Not that I didn't like his broad shoulders, but sometimes his presence felt overwhelming. Dryads had some kinship with the Duannae, and I knew that their kind worshiped different trees. Timberfoot had to be an oak. There was majesty in his bearing, and confidence, and a just a hint of playfulness.

He waited for me at the bottom of the staircase with a relaxed, easy stance, not fussing with his collar or cuffs. Well, well. The dryad was no stranger to court dress. He continued to surprise me.

His gaze met mine and held it as I descended. Then he took my hand, his callouses rubbing against mine.

"You look lovely. I told you there was a real princess under all that dirt."

"Thank you." Once, before my years on Terra, I would have bristled at that double-edged compliment, but now I accepted it. I had been dirty. And I was a princess. The two weren't mutually exclusive.

"You clean up nicely too, Mr. Timberfoot."

He leaned in as if to kiss me then showed me his teeth. "My friends call me Tim."

"Is that what we are? Friends?"

"Friends, allies, dance partners. Whatever you wish."

He held out his arm, and I let him lead me to the dance floor.

"You don't strike me as a Tim. I think I'll stick with Timberfoot."

"Whatever the lady wishes."

As we moved through the crowd of courtiers, a wave of murmurs followed us. Some recognized me and spread the word that the princess had returned. No one intercepted us, but I greeted polite nods with courteous, if distant, smiles.

Timberfoot was light on his feet for his size. His right hand held me firmly at my waist. His left gripped my fingers lightly as we twirled among the colorful court dandies. The women wore elaborate gowns, as if trying to outdo each other with lace and baubles. Unlike human males, Duannan men adored color, and many of them outshone their dance partners. And my imp attendant was right. Men and woman both wore glamors to hide sagging middles and graying hair. I keened their magics as we bumped against them on the dance floor.

At the corner of the hall, an elf quartet played traditional Duannan music—a complicated and lilting song that no one could really dance to properly. Pixies added their own tinkle to the mix as they flitted through the dancers. Chandeliers hung like icicles from the ceiling, and the fae lanterns at their hearts cast the room in a soft yellow glow. Ice sculptures adorned every table around the dance floor. These ranged from horned beasts of the Wild Hunt to elfin lovers entwined in risqué embraces—all hewn from ice be-spelled not to melt until the dancing ended. Below the sculptures, glowing flutes of wine and mead were stacked in pyramids. Soon the glasses would be empty, and the dancers would find secluded spots in the shadows to end the evening with their lovers.

"So what is this ball for?" Timberfoot asked.

I shrugged. "It must be Tuesday."

He cocked his head at an angle. "What does that mean?"

"It means there's always a ball at the Winter Court. They don't need a reason. But in this case, I believe it's the lesser ball leading up to the Solstice festival."

"Lesser ball? You mean it gets fancier?"

"You have no idea."

The quartet finished their song and started a new, more solemn piece. Timberfoot snugged me a bit closer. My hip bumped up against the long line of his solid thigh.

I opened my mouth to say something and shut it again. I didn't want words intruding on the moment. My world was coming to an end, but I couldn't do anything about it until the Council sought me out. Instead, I could have this moment. I leaned my head against his shoulder and let the music dictate the rhythm to our bodies.

"Leighna! I heard you were back. I almost didn't believe it was true."

The voice grated against my thoughts, jarring me from my place of calm. I moved away from the tall pillar of strength that was Timberfoot to greet Eamon—ex-lover, ex-friend and general in the king's army. His post was a formality only. He'd never seen a day of combat in his life.

"Eamon. Merry meet." I bent my knees in a minuscule curtsy.

"Merry meet." He raised one eyebrow at me. Somehow Eamon could make even the simplest greeting sound biting and sarcastic. "May I cut in for the next dance?"

The song ended. Just my luck. The band struck up another, slower piece. More bitter luck. Why couldn't they play a nice polka so I could keep Eamon's grabby-grabby hands at arm's length?

I plastered a smile on my face. "Of course."

Timberfoot bowed and went to stand by an ice sculpture of two crows watching over a sleeping maid.

Eamon turned us around the dance floor with more vigor than the song demanded, and I lost sight of the dryad. Eamon was a flawless dancer. His family came from the Sidhe Clan, and he had the tall grace of that line. Blond hair swept back from his face in a perfect wave. His features were fine, with wide cheekbones and deep-set blue eyes. Eyes that I once thought sparkled with humor and love. Now I saw they were chips of ice merely reflecting the world around them.

People were looking at us. It was no secret that we were once betrothed. Breaking up with him had been the hardest thing I ever did. Everyone approved our match—my parents, his parents, the Council and the people. He wasn't a prince, but his lineage went back as far as mine. The commoners saw a fairytale in our wedding. Escaping the disappointment of an entire nation was why I left for Terra.

"Queen Reneni had an interesting tale to tell the Council just now." He twirled us through the throng of dancers then leaned in to whisper. "Do you truly believe there is a demon in Underhill?"

"Yes." I turned away from his piercing gaze.

"I see your years away haven't let you grow up any." He laughed. It was a bitter sound. Not for the first time, I wondered what was broken inside Eamon. It certainly wasn't our canceled wedding. He'd been damaged long before that.

I pushed away and stopped dancing. Inertia kept his feet going for a moment before he realized I stood still.

"Horak is here," I said. "He will attack where the magic burns brightest. He feeds on it." I waved a hand to encompass the fae chandeliers and glamored courtiers, each with their magic burning bright. This place was a demon smorgasbord. "You need to bring the army home. And you need to do it now."

"On who's authority? A flighty princess who abandoned her people ten years ago? Ten years is a long time, Princess. Long enough for you to lose your influence."

I gritted my teeth. He didn't have to like me. He just had to believe. "Gander was there too. He'll tell you."

"That old dwarf couldn't find his own arse unless it was at the bottom of an ale pot."

The music died and a herald stepped onto the dais. He put a flute to his lips and played the strident march that announced the king's entrance. Everyone turned to the grand doors at the far end of the hall.

And I saw my father for the first time in ten years.

King Irilahiec the Great had ruled in Underhill for six-hundred years. His nickname was the Duannan Bear. And once he had stood as tall and barrel-chested as a grizzly. Now he was shrunken and gray, more like an angry badger than a bear. Dancers moved out of the way, making an aisle for him. He held Mother's arm as they strode to the dais at the front of the hall where two thrones waited. Elaborate friezes depicting great heroes of Duannan history decorated the wall behind the thrones.

Father dropped heavily onto his seat and seemed to disappear into his fur-lined cloak.

Mother stood before her throne, the picture of regal beauty and grace. A server came forward with glowing flutes of wine. She held hers up. "A toast!" A pixie zipped around her head, but the queen was too stately to swat it. More servers rushed through the crowd, making sure everyone had a glass.

Mother waited a moment, then said, "To family and friends, gathered here—"

"Where's my daughter?" Father roused in his seat. "Leighna? Where's Leighna?"

I stood frozen in the shadows. I didn't like the limelight at the best of times, and Father's demand broke protocol. Toasts came first, then guests were honored. Then the Council. Family came last. My nursemaids and tutors had droned this routine into me since I was a child fidgeting at the endless processions.

"You said Leighna was here." Father's voice sank into a whine. A loud whine. Mother tried to shush him, but he wouldn't have it. "I want to see my daughter."

"I'm here, Father." I stepped into the light.

"There you are!" The king rose from his seat and tripped down the few stairs to meet me on the dance floor. Someone gasped at this new breach in etiquette. Murmurs slithered through the crowd. And suddenly my father swept me up in his big bear arms like I was a little girl again—like we weren't in a formal and very public setting.

"Leighna! You've been gone for weeks! You should not make a father worry so."

It had been years, not weeks, since I last set eyes on him.

"I missed you too, Father." I kissed his leathery soft cheek.

He held my shoulders in his meaty hands. While he studied me, I studied him. The skin on his face hung in jowls, and his beard was patchy. His eyes, once as sharp as a falcon's, were hazed with cataracts.

He squeezed my arms. "It's good to have you home. You look well. Strong."

"Thank you. You look…" I fought against unruly tears, but Father didn't notice.

"And Eamon!" His voice boomed over the now-silent crowd. "You're taking care of Leighna, I see. Wonderful. I knew you two would work things out."

I squirmed out of my father's grip. He'd forgotten that by breaking up with Eamon I insulted his family and nearly caused a civil war. Eamon's post as general and advisor to the king was a consolation, a way to fix the rift.

Eamon affected a perfect bow. "You are looking well, Sire."

"Ha! Never stronger!" Father thumped a fist against his chest.

Mother had recovered from her aborted toast and appeared beside us.

"Look, Rene! Leighna is home in time for Solstice." Father leaned into me and said in an over-loud whisper. "Your brothers will be glad to see you too."

I closed my eyes and wished for this moment to end. Alvar my younger brother was away, serving in the army. My elder brother, Irlac, was dead these twenty years.

"Get the music going," my mother hissed to Eamon. He smirked and bowed again before heading toward the quartet. The music started up and dancers reluctantly moved onto the floor.

Mother gave me a sad smile, a sort of apology, and took Father's hand. "Come now, my love. Let's get you a glass of wine. And your legs must be tired." Father made a mewling noise as she led him away.

I felt lost.

I had expected a chill welcome on my return, but I hadn't expected this. The father I had loved and admired was gone. The brilliant tactician, the shrewd diplomat, the beloved leader…they were all gone. The grizzly was a gray ghost.

Couples whirled around me, their bright dress like the plumes of fluttering birds. I looked for an escape and found Timberfoot.

"Come on," he pulled me to him. His hands held me in a perfect Waltz pose, and he whirled us effortlessly through the crowd. At the doors to the balcony he let me go.

"Thank you," I said. "I need to get out of here."

We stepped into the cool evening air, but I had only a moment to steady my shuddering breath.

The music came to a screeching end. A shout penetrated the balcony doors.

"Something's wrong." I clenched Timberfoot's fingers and pulled him back inside.

The ballroom was in chaos. Instead of dancing, women now wept in the arms of their partners. A full guard of twelve soldiers surrounded a scout in a torn and bloody uniform who stood before the king's dais.

I grabbed a passing server. "What's happening."

"Ill news, milady. The garrison at Saguaro has been overrun."

So the Council could no longer contain the news. War had come to Underhill.

"Did they say who the enemy is?"

The server pitched from foot to foot, clearly uncomfortable. "Not sure, milady. I heard them say it was spiders. But that makes no sense."

To this poor man it made no sense. There were no vermin in Underhill.

To me it made perfect sense.

"And the town? Did anyone get away?"

"The scout says only a few dozen. They're an hour behind him." The server slipped away before I could ask him more.

A few dozen people. A thousand soldiers, plus an entire town had fallen to Horak's trolls.

"We must speak to the Council." I gripped Timberfoot's hand, and we pushed through the crowd toward the king and queen who now sat like alabaster statues on their thrones.

The scout still stood among the king's honor guard. He was so exhausted two soldiers held him up by the arms. He looked like a prisoner, and when the soldiers dragged him away, my worst fears came to light.

They would bury this story. The Council would gloss over the deaths, pretend everything was normal.

I wouldn't have it.

Eamon shot me an angry glance when I hiked my skirts and marched up the stairs to stand beside my parents. But he couldn't protest, not with the dozen courtiers pulling at his sleeves and shouting into his face for answers.

"People!" I laced my voice with power to be heard over the rumbling crowd. "You may remember me as a spoiled daughter who ran when I didn't get my way."

Stunned faces turned to me.

"I have spent the last years learning to be real. I stand before you wearing no glamor." My voice dropped to its normal pitch. "I speak to you in my own voice. I am no longer a princess." I smiled sadly at my father. His expression was blank. "At least I am no longer just a princess. On Terra I became a warrior. And I advise you from a place of experience—experience won by fighting demons. Horak is here."

A murmur rippled through the room. I spoke over it.

"Horak is a demon of the worst kind. He feeds on magic." I looked pointedly around the room. "Especially life magic. He craves you, the beautifully magical creatures of Underhill most of all. And he won't leave here until he has obliterated us all. There is only one way to stop—"

Shouting voices cut me off. People surged toward the dais and the remaining honor guard had trouble holding them back.

"There is no need for panic!" Eamon's voice cut through the noise. He jumped the stairs to stand beside me.

"The princess exaggerates the situation."

"What about the garrison?" Someone shouted from the crowd.

"What about Saguaro?" Came another angry voice.

Eamon held out his hands, placating the crowd.

"Be calm. These are only rumors. We, the Council, will get to the bottom of these wild stories. Please, enjoy the music."

I keened a zing of magic from Eamon. He waved a hand, and the quartet began a shaky waltz.

"This is crazy! You have to listen!" I shouted, but the courtiers began to dance again, like glittering automatons. Servers flitted through the revelers giving out more glasses of glowing wine.

I waved my arms but no one even looked my way.

"They can no longer hear you or see you." Eamon wore a smug expression. I stepped to the edge of the dais and felt it. A ward protected us from the crowd. I pressed my fingers to the invisible barrier. It gave a bit like thick pudding, but it was a solid construct.

I wheeled around. Father had fallen asleep on his throne. I addressed my mother.

"Why do the king and queen need a ward in their own hall?"

She rose and took my hand. "Not just a ward. It's a glamor." She glanced at Father who looked like a shadow of himself.

"No one should see their king in this state. So we put on balls and let them dance in front of a glamor. All they see is an aged, but alert king smiling down on his subjects."

I ran a hand over my face. Every molecule of my body cried out for a rest.

How long had this been going on? Why hadn't I bothered to visit? I should have taken my place as heir long ago. Now it might be too late. No one would take orders from a stranger. But I had to try.

"Mother, listen to me. Bring the army home. Horak will come here first."

Eamon made a sound like a snort. "This is ridiculous! She has no proof."

Queen Reneni turned to him. "You forget your place, Eamon. The Princess's word carries more weight than yours. Remember that. Now go convene the Council. We will be in shortly to speak with them."

Eamon didn't like being dismissed. The muscles on his jaws pumped as he ground his teeth.

"Yes, milady." He bowed low, but his eyes never left mine, and they flashed with angry fire.

Mother clapped her hands and attendants came to help Father back to his rooms. She walked toward the back of the dais and ran her hand along the wall. A door opened, its edges artfully hidden by the lines of the plaster frieze.

"Come." She beckoned. "We have much to do."

I glanced at the dancing crowd. The glamor was a one-way window. They might not see us, but I could see them perfectly. In the crowd of outrageous costumes, Timberfoot's solemn dark figure stood out. He searched the faces, looking for me.

"No." I reached my mother and hugged her. "You go. The Council will never listen to me. Make them face the truth."

"What will you do?"

"I closed Saguaro Door, but I was too late." I took a deep breath, trying not to focus on my failure. "Now I'm going to close every door to Underhill."

Mother's eyes widened as she understood the implications of that plan.

"You want to trap him here."

"Yes. You need to convince the council to evacuate Underhill. Send as many people through the doors before as you can. Before I close them. Then bring the army home and protect the city. Horak won't be able to resist it. He'll ravage the smaller towns first, gaining strength and rebuilding his army. But his goal will be Winter City. Make a stand here. Throw everything you have at him."

"Will it be enough?"

"It has to be."

Mother hugged me fiercely, but we both knew the truth. There was nothing in our arsenal—magic or otherwise—that could stop a demon. We could only hope to keep him occupied long enough for me to set the trap. I had eight doors to close. And I would start with the one under this palace.

I STEPPED OFF the dais and startled a pair of dancers as I suddenly emerged from the glamor.

Timberfoot saw me from across the hall and his demeanor changed from worry to bulldozer. He pushed through the crowd, ignoring curses and protests.

"Where have you been?"

"It doesn't matter. I need your help. Will you come?"

"Of course."

"We'll need Gander too."

At this time of the evening I knew where I'd find my old tutor.

We left the main hall, but instead of heading up the stairs to the guest quarters, we turned toward the servants' wing. These halls were bare stone, but wide and clean. Servers rushed back and forth bringing out the midnight buffet. No one stopped us questioned our purpose.

I found Gander asleep on a bench in the kitchen. A flagon of ale had tipped over, making a puddle on the floor beside him. His snores reverberated over the kitchen bustle. Servers and cooks worked around the sleeping dwarf.

I kicked his bench. He snorted and fell to the ground.

"I'm awake." He came to all fours and sniffed the empty flagon before standing upright.

"Oh, Princess. I did not expect—"

"Did you hear the news?"

He scratched his beard and stretched.

"What news."

"A scout came in from Saguaro. The garrison is lost. The town too. We'll be getting an influx of refugees any time now." At least I hoped we would. We'd be lucky if Horak left anyone alive.

Gander was awake now.

"Did you speak to the Council?" I asked.

"Bunch of arse holes." He patted down his clothes, found his knife, unsheathed it and re-sheathed it as if making sure it was still there. "They won't act until Horak sends them an embossed invitation to their own funerals."

I sighed. "That's what I thought. We're not waiting for them. I'm going to close the doors."

"What doors?" The dwarf pulled on his beard.

"All of them. Starting with the Winter Door. Are you in?"

"Oh, aye." He picked up his flagon and shook the last drops into his mouth. "All right, then. Let me get my kit. I'll meet you in the underground."

The tunnels under the palace were dark. The only light came from fae lanterns in sconces on the stone walls. Several were burned out, so we walked through gaps of near complete darkness along the hallway. The air was stale. Gravel crackled under our feet, sounding unnaturally loud in the closed space.

Gander waited at the end of a forgotten hallway. A stout wooden door reinforced with black iron bands blocked the way.

"Is that the door to Duanna?" Timberfoot kept his voice low. This place seemed to demand reverence.

"No." I pushed the door, and it opened on well-oiled hinges. Inside a small room was empty. A shimmering portal filled one wall.

"That's Duanna," I said. Beyond the portal, I could see the frozen lands of my ancestors. In the distance, sharply peaked mountains scraped the sky. Just beyond the door, odd structures of ice rose out of a snow-packed ground. A city of ice. My father's Winter Palace was built to mimic the ancient cities of Duanna, but it could not compare to their beauty. Our old world was abandoned now. There was desolation in its emptiness but also beauty.

"Why did the Duannae leave?" Timberfoot had snuck up behind me, and I startled at his words. I hugged my arms, though the cold from Duanna didn't penetrate the portal.

"The usual. War. Famine. Covetous men and women who thought they deserved more than they were given."

I pointed to the silver statue standing beside the door—a queenly woman dressed in a flowing gown with her faithful wolf at her side.

"That is Seana and Bane, her wolf-guide. She was the first queen of Underhill. She convinced an entire world to follow her. I wish I had her charisma."

Timberfoot slipped his hand in mine and squeezed. "You did what you could."

"Seana was a great sorcerer. She weaved the spell to open this door. That magic was lost when she died. But her legacy remained. Seana promised our people that they could always return to Duanna, if they wanted. The door has remained open for eons. And now I must break her promise."

"Can't your people return now? Flee to old Duanna to escape Horak?"

I shook my head. "It's a dead planet. If we are going to save even a few

Duannae, they must go to Terra. We will have to brave the human war and hope a few of our people survive."

It would be hard for the spoiled courtiers of Underhill who had known nothing but lives of leisure. But the Duannae weren't just courtiers. We were soldiers, bakers, weavers, storytellers and more. The fluff might get chaffed away, but the stalk would survive to flourish.

Because Duanna Door was the first door built between the two worlds, its generator was on the other side. Gander jumped through the gate and came back unrolling a large bobbin of string. Frost laced his mustache and brows, and his face was already red with the cold. He left the bobbin on the floor in front of the door and unsheathed his sword. It let out a quiet but shrill shriek as he primed it. The magic was strong in the palace, and it didn't take long. He held the blade to the string and ignited it with a spark. Not string, I now understood. It was a wick.

The wick rippled like a snake as the flame fizzled through the door.

Gander stuck his finger in his ears. "Hold onto yer chestnuts!"

Timberfoot and I jumped back. An explosion lit the Duannan sky. The portal slammed shut.

Gander looked up at me with sad eyes. "One more down. Seven doors to go."

SHENNONGJIA DOOR

THE ONLY JOYFUL part of my return to Underhill was Segrid. When we turned our backs on Winter City, I rode out on the seventeen-hand buck with a rack of antlers as wide as my outstretched arms. Segrid hadn't left the palace grounds in years because none of the grooms could saddle him. The first few miles were rough going for both of us, but he soon remembered his manners and I regained my seat.

That summer and fall, Timberfoot, Gander and I ranged across Underhill and closed three more doors. During these months, we spied refugees from all over. Some were heading toward Winter City. Others streamed through the doors, willing to take their chances with the human war. Twice we hid from roving bands of troll spiders, advance scouts for Horak's army.

As the Terran Winter Solstice approached, we closed in on Shennongjia Door. We were tired, saddle-weary and nearly out of supplies. We came to the end of the forest as the blue sky faded to gray. Moss Village was only another few hours' ride, and the door lay beyond that. I didn't know this terrain, so we camped on the edge of the trees and would make for the village in the morning.

Timberfoot unsaddled the horses and brushed them down. I pulled off Segrid's saddle, laid my head against his sturdy withers and sank my love into him.

"Thank you for carrying me another day, my friend." The buck let out a rumbling purr. I stepped back and he bounded into the trees.

"I can't believe you just let him go like that," Timberfoot said. "How can you be sure he'll come back?"

"It's hard to explain. Segrid has been part of my life since I was a baby. He was gifted to me by a powerful elf-witch and she bonded us. Even when I went to Terra, I could always feel a thread tying me to him." I paused, trying to find the words. "He fills my heart. I guess you would call it love."

Timberfoot watched me with open surprise. I turned away and pretended to fuss with the saddlebags. When had I become so hardened—so cynical—that speaking of love embarrassed me? The Duannae did not shy from emotion. We believed in grand gestures—in love and in war. But admitting my feelings to this man made me squirm.

Timberfoot went back to brushing his gelding, giving me a moment to collect myself.

"I understand what you mean," he said without looking at me. "I lost my family, but I never stopped feeling them."

"Your entire family?"

His eyes turned into liquid emeralds, and he gave one curt nod. I didn't know what to say. I laid a hand on his shoulder and felt muscles bunching and pulling as he stroked the horse.

"There isn't anything left to eat!" Gander's voice cut through the quiet bubble that had been building around us. He rifled through our saddle bags, yanking out and scattering our carefully packed supplies.

"I'll go." It was a relief to sling my bow over my shoulder. "I can forage. Maybe find mushrooms for dinner."

"I'd rather you use those arrows and catch me a nice steak," Gander grumbled. But I didn't take him seriously. These forests were sacred and he knew it. The animals here were all descendants of the Wild Hunt. I'd just as soon roast Segrid over the fire than kill a Hunt beast.

An hour later, I returned to camp with a flat-head mushroom, big enough to satisfy Gander's steak craving. I'd also found wild carrots and leeks. It would be a feast.

Timberfoot had started a fire while I was gone. Gander was already asleep leaning against the bedrolls.

"I guess he wasn't much help setting up camp," I said.

"Leave him be." Timberfoot fed another log to the fire. "He's earned his rest. I don't know how he finds the courage to close those doors. Each one seems more painful than the last."

It was true. Even in sleep, Gander didn't look restful. His snores lacked enthusiasm. And his skin was a sickly white, hanging from his face like it was detaching from his bones.

I woke him when the meal was ready. He didn't hide his disappointment when I handed him a plate.

"Don't worry," I said. "We'll kit up in Moss tomorrow."

Gander stuffed the mushroom in his mouth with dirty fingers, then wiped them on his beard. Before I had even finished my meal, he was tucked up and snoring again.

"Help me get him settled for the night." I tried hefting the sleeping dwarf and Timberfoot came to help me. We unrolled his bed and left him to his fitful sleep.

The light had faded to gray, and we sat before the fire. I leaned back and stared at the empty sky.

"On Terra, a clear sky like this would be full of stars," I said.

Timberfoot leaned back too, bringing him up against my shoulder. I liked the strong weight of him beside me.

"Do you miss it?"

"Yes. It's funny. When I was on Terra, I was terribly homesick. Now, I'm home and I wish I could go back."

He made a small noise of agreement.

"You're not a man of many words, are you?"

"No." He turned to me. A half-grin played at the edge of his mouth. "Does that bother you?"

"We've been riding together for weeks, and I feel like we barely know each other."

We were close enough to kiss. His eyes ranged down to my lips and back up again. I licked my lips as if tasting his thoughts.

"What do you want to know?"

"About your family."

He froze. I felt him tense.

Stupid, stupid! Why couldn't I just let a moment be?

He sat up, hooked his arms around his knees and stared into the fire. "There's not much to know."

I touched his back and he flinched.

"I'm sorry. I didn't mean to pry. But it was odd to find a dryad in the Arizona desert."

"A last ditch effort to locate them."

"Who?"

"My wife and daughter."

Oh. I sat up too, scolding myself inwardly. I shouldn't be thinking of tasting him in any way. Not with Horak on the loose. Once before I had put Timberfoot ahead of my good reason. And for that, I'd let a demon into our world. Now my guilt forced me into this mad mission. Until I closed all the doors, I had no room in my life for anything else.

I straightened my shirt and brushed a bit of dirt from my knee.

After a moment, he continued.

"I wanted to ask…about the doors. How are they made?" That question had come out of nowhere, and he saw my hesitation to answer. "I mean, we closed doors to Terra and Duanna. Are there other doors to other worlds?"

He sat with his legs drawn up to his chest and clasped his hands between his knees. The magic was strong in the palace.

"Why do you want to know?"

"My wife and daughter. They left Terra for Asgard. But that was many years ago. Long before the war." He rubbed a hand over his eyes, then through his hair, leaving his curls sticking up every which way. "I heard a rumor that an Aesir was in Tucson. She was my last chance at finding the road to Asgard."

"Did you find her?"

He shook his head. "Tucson was in chaos by the time I got there. Then Horak appeared and…I ran. I thought maybe there was a way to get to Asgard from here."

I shook my head. "Seana was a powerful witch. No one alive today can replicate her spell."

"And the doors to Terra?"

"The first one was an accident." I searched my memories. "Gander could tell you more. But if I remember correctly, it was caused by a freak magic storm. Like a lightning bolt that struck the right place and the right time. After that, a strong enough fae working with a magically gifted human could open others, but it hasn't been done since my grandfather's generation. And I wouldn't even know where to begin opening a door to Asgard. I'm sorry." I covered his hand in mine. He shot me a small smile.

"It was a slim chance anyway." He tossed another stick into the fire and we watched the sparks dance into the sky like fairy lights. "Even if I found her, my daughter would be a woman now. Hard to believe. I only got to hold her once. After she was born, I went on an emergency diplomatic mission for my clan. To the oreads, in the north. You know them?"

I shook my head.

"Cousins, of a sort, to the dryads. Oreads are always itching for a fight. This time it was over land. I tried to smooth things over without bloodshed. They took me prisoner, demanded ransom in the form of land rights. Of course, they don't know my mother. She doesn't bargain." He smiled sadly. "They only let me go because the human war had destroyed their city. By then, I'd been a prisoner for over twenty years. I came home to find my family gone. I've been looking for them ever since. But now," he fisted his hands, then opened them wide as if freeing memories, "it's time I let them go."

Unlike the forests of Terra, this one was quiet at night. There were no predators calling out their hunt songs. The only sounds were the crackle of the flames and Gander's rumbling snore. We watched the fire in silence. Timberfoot held my hand. His thumb circled the fleshy part of my palm, over and over, as if he needed the reassurance of touch as much as I did. Eventually I fell asleep leaning against my giant dryad.

In the early hours, my keening pinged something in the trees.

I sat up straight. The fire still smoked. Timberfoot was asleep beside me, but my movement woke him.

"What is it?"

I held up my hand as I keened the magic of the forest. Something big approached, not moving fast, but coming straight for us.

The horses whickered and pranced, pulling on the leads that tied them in place.

"Put out the fire." I rose and went to wake Gander. He snorted and growled as he sat up.

"What's the meaning—"

"Shush." I cocked my thumb at the woods. We could all hear it now. The cracking of branches as something or someone stumbled through the underbrush.

Timberfoot smothered the fire with the pile of dirt we had put aside for such an emergency. I peered into the shadows.

"Spider?" His voice was barely above a breath.

"I don't think so." Troll spiders were more stealthy. Whatever was coming sounded injured, desperate and lost. Why else would they clamber through the underbrush like a drunken bear instead of using the path?

"Take the horses," I said to Gander. The dwarf tried to calm the agitated beasts. Timberfoot and I stood on the edge of the forest knives out.

A figure burst from the trees.

It was a boy. No, a full grown man, but hunched over, holding his stomach. As he got closer, he tripped and sprawled on the ground. His hands and face were caked with blood and dirt, his shirt soaked in a dark stain.

He saw us and tried to scramble backward.

"It's okay!" I held out my hands. "We won't hurt you."

His eyes were round and wild. I could see now my first assessment had been right. He was a teenaged human.

"Spiders!" The word hissed from him. He lay back and closed his eyes. I ran to crouch at his side. His hands fell away. I lifted his shirt, tugging gently where it stuck to the wound. The boy had passed out and didn't even flinch.

A deep gash scored his abdomen. It leaked black blood sluggishly. Sweat soaked his face and hair.

Timberfoot covered the wound with his hands. I felt a zing of magic. He was trying to heal him. But after a moment, he met my eye and gave a small shake of his head. He let his hands drop away. The wound still oozed.

Gander came with a canteen and we propped him up. The boy opened his eyes for a moment as cool water touched his lips.

I gripped his hand. "Where did you see the spiders?"

"M…Moss."

The village was ahead of us. Poor kid got turned around in the forest and didn't realize he was heading back to the home of his nightmares.

The effort to speak was too much, and he collapsed. His eyes shut and they didn't open again.

We buried him beside the forest. He wasn't the first body we buried on the road, and he wouldn't be the last. The little mound of soil that marked his grave was just another monument to my failure. And it spurred me to make sure I wouldn't fail again.

For the next several miles we rode through a plain of heather-like grasses, each of us lost to our private thoughts.

"You didn't tell me you were a healer." I side-eyed the tall dryad who rode beside me.

"Shush!"

"Don't shush me!" I didn't add "I'm a princess," but we both heard it. I rubbed my eyes to hide the blush burning my cheeks. Only a few months in Underhill and I was already returning to old habits. I blamed it on lack of sleep.

"I'm listening to the grasses," he said. "They're not as eloquent as trees. Harder to understand."

We rode for several minutes. And while I keened the expansive magic of the grass plains, the only sound I heard was the gentle clop of hooves on soft ground.

"And I'm not a healer." Timberfoot gave me a sharp look. "It's a minor talent. I can treat scrapes and bruises. My mother is better, but she's a ranger too and has little time to devote to the gentler arts."

"A ranger? That's like dryad royalty, isn't it?"

"Dryads have no royalty. Many see my mother as a leader, but she's not a queen."

"I see."

"Does that matter?" A slow grin spread across Timberfoot's face. He wanted to know: could a princess ever fall in love with a commoner?

"Makes no difference to me."

"Indeed." His lips twitched as if he held in a laugh, and something that I hadn't even realized was sleeping awoke in me.

For so many weeks we'd insulated ourselves in a cocoon of desperation and fear. It was the only way to stay focused on a mission that would doom so many of my people. Now a hint of secret happiness penetrated the cocoon. It was like I had a tiny rose blooming in the middle of a harsh winter, and even if I could never show it to anyone else, I could cherish it.

Timberfoot reached across and took my hand, and we rode in companionable silence. I could almost pretend we were out for an afternoon ride without a care in the world.

"So, what are they saying?" I asked.

"Who?"

"The grasses. You said you were listening to the grasses."

He sighed. "They say there is no ambush ahead."

"That's good isn't it?"

"Yes." His wide mouth dipped into a frown. "But there's death on the wind. A lot of it."

I shivered and pulled my cloak more tightly around me.

The path dipped into a valley. In every direction the whispering grasses spread like a yellow blanket to the horizon, but ahead, smoke rose in a dark cloud. We no longer needed the grasses to warn us. The wind reeked of burned flesh.

Moss Village was on fire.

Even though I expected it, the carnage in Moss was worse than I could have imagined, and I'd lived through the Flood Wars on Terra. I could imagine a lot.

Houses were burned. Scorched corpses were sprawled in the streets as if they'd tried to crawl away from the ruins of their homes. Blood pooled in the village square like it had rained from the sky. Bodies had been left to rot. On Terra vermin would savage them, but Underhill had no rats or insects, so the bodies were strangely and horrifyingly intact. A few of Horak's spider minions lay dead where villagers had fought back.

"There aren't enough bodies here," I said. Moss village was home to nearly a thousand souls. The bodies numbered in the hundreds.

"These are the lucky ones." Timberfoot stared at a charred corpse. And the horror of his assumptions nearly choked me. He was right. These *were* the lucky ones. Spider trolls cut them down during the first assault. The others—the missing—were taken alive so that Horak could drink their magic, bolstering his own power so he could remake his army. He was probably sitting on in his camp right now, sucking the life out of Duannan men and women, chucking away their lifeless wrappers.

"Look for survivors." I shut down the coal of rage, remorse and terror glowing in my gut. We had a job to do.

An hour later we'd found no one alive. We piled as many bodies as we could inside one cottage. Timberfoot took a lit brand from one of the fires still burning and sparked the thatched roof.

Good. Let it all burn.

Our pace slowed as we entered Thorny Downs on the other side of Moss. Low grasses turned into thick, tall stalks with heavy seedpods that bent westward, then north, then west again in an elaborate and unending dance choreographed by the winds.

I broke the trail, trampling the stalks flat. Gander and Timberfoot followed in a line. After an hour, Timberfoot took my place to give Segrid a rest. I brought up the rear and watched Gander list in his saddle as the day wore on. When his pony stumbled on a stone, he snorted awake, fumbled for his wineskin and cursed heroically when he found it empty. I tossed him my canteen. He drank and made a face.

"Water? Are you trying to kill me? A man needs ale to survive this journey. Or at least wine."

"Water," I said. "You need your wits about you. We'll be at the door soon."

He grumbled again, but it was all bluster. His patient pony plodded on and soon Gander was asleep in the saddle again, clutching his precious sword, the only weapon that could save the Duannae.

"He cannot keep this up." Timberfoot's voice floated to me like a breath of wind. I felt it too. Gander's essence was off, like he was out of phase with the universe. Closing the gates had a price. He left a bit of himself behind with each door. I knew my old teacher well enough to recognize that his complaining masked a deep unease.

Three more doors. I hugged those words to my heart. We had to close three more doors. We had to survive. Then I would make sure Gander got the rest he deserved.

I felt a change in the air and shouted, "Hold!"

The winds died. The grasses stilled. I shielded my eyes and searched in the direction where I keened a tingle of dark magic.

I pulled my blade. Timberfoot came up beside me. He had only his short utility knife as a weapon.

"You should have picked up a sword in Moss," I said.

He shrugged. "Dryads are not warriors. We avoid bloodshed." He held out his fists. Each one was bigger than both of mine together. "But I'll use these if I have to."

Terrific. I hoped he'd have my back, but I was used to fending for myself if I had to.

"Just stay behind me then."

Segrid snorted and shuffled sideways.

"Easy." My fingers twined in his thick fur.

Ahead and at an angle to our company, something parted the grasses, something sprinting low and fast. Something that tasted of brimstone and fire.

"Run!" I swung Segrid around and pushed him into a lope before I realized my mistake. Gander's pony could barely see over the grass heads. He would never make it through the Downs alone. But when I turned back for the dwarf, I saw him secured to the saddle in front of Timberfoot. And the dryad was gaining fast.

A spider troll leapt from the grass and latched onto Timberfoot's head. A scream lodged in my throat as a second troll dashed under Segrid's legs. The buck reared and I plummeted to the hard-packed ground. The impact left me fighting for air, staring at the impossible blue sky. A troll stomped on my chest, crushing my already breathless lungs. Its man-like hands circled my neck—squeezing, squeezing—while spider claws snapped like scissors in front of my nose. I scrabbled at my belt until I freed my blade and drove it into the spider's eye. Yellow blood splashed my face. The claws clacked and spasmed, but it fell dead. I gripped the hilt of my knife with slick and shaky hands. The dead spider stared at me with dead eyes. I thrust off the carcass and rolled into the shadows to suck air.

The Downs were silent. Timberfoot loomed over two more carcasses. Dozens of cuts scored his bare arms, and he wiped his hands on his pants, smearing them with yellow blood.

I rose on rubber legs. "I thought you weren't a warrior."

"I said I avoid bloodshed, not that I wouldn't fight. It was you or the spiders. No contest." He grinned and I felt like a summer sun shone on me. A real Terran sun.

MY WARM FEELING lasted only until we rounded up the mounts. Gander's pony was dead, its stomach slashed open by spider claws. A gash on Segrid's left flank oozed blood. The wound could be fatal if untreated.

"I can heal him, but I need more." Timberfoot waved a hand at the bleak landscape. "I need trees."

Segrid's eyes were sharp and glassy, and his head drooped. I glanced backward at the endless plains. The forest was already a day's ride behind us.

"The gate." My gaze turned to the center of Thorny Downs where Shennongjia Door opened onto a vast forest in China. Even before the wars, magic pooled in the shadows among Shennongjia's great boles. It was the perfect place for a dryad healing.

Segrid couldn't hold my weight. I walked him through the grasses. Timberfoot led the gelding with Gander on his back.

The army had abandoned the garrison at Shennongjia. It was too remote for refugees, so we were alone. Gander set up his amplifier. I stepped through the gate, pulling Segrid behind me. Timberfoot planted his two feet on Terran soil and breathed in the loamy air. He seemed bigger here, like the tree spirits filled him to overflowing.

Segrid was near fainting. I pulled off the hastily wrapped bandage. His wound still leaked, and I keened the sour bite of life seeping out with the blood.

Timberfoot laid his hands across the gash. Segrid shied, but I held him firm.

"My sweet boy. My brave, strong boy," I cooed. The buck snorted, breath steaming in the chill air. I laid my cheek against his neck, breathing in his wild scent. Segrid had carried me since I was a girl. He'd been the only bearable thing about coming home to Underhill. And now, one way or another, I'd lose him.

The dryad's magic swelled. It sang with joy and the trees echoed him, eager to play their part in his spell. His hands glowed. Or maybe that was my keening eye interpreting the magic. Timberfoot's well of power was much deeper than he let on.

The wound closed. Segrid snorted and danced away. This time, I let him go.

"Find peace, my friend. You've done your duty." He butted me with his velvety nose, and I held him for one last moment. Then he turned and dashed over a bramble before disappearing into the forest.

I wrenched my heart away from following him.

"That wasn't a random strike in the Downs." Timberfoot glanced back at the glowing portal. "They were hunting us."

"I know." Horak was worried about the closing doors. We were slowly cutting off his escape routes. He'd sent his spiders to stop us. It was another reason I let Segrid go. We would be a less conspicuous party without the Wild Hunt beast. But we wouldn't be safe until we stood on Terra for good.

Only three doors left.

I shot one last glance at the shadows that had swallowed Segrid. Then I turned back to Underhill and the Shennongjia Door.

London Door

THE GARRISON AT London Door consisted of only a few soldiers too old or too wounded to leave. Timberfoot and I left Gander with them to set up his casting and stepped through the door to London. I wanted to gauge the effect of the Flood Wars that still raged on Terra.

Most doors sat on out-of-the-way sites where a human had to be persistent or utterly lost to find them. London Door opened in the heart of the city, on a site that had once been sacred to the Duannae. Now it was owned by a family of fae hoteliers who'd been serving as gatekeepers for a thousand years. I'd met them many decades past, when the new young Queen of England invited my parents to visit.

But the hotel had collapsed around the door, and the gatekeepers were nowhere in sight. Timberfoot and I spent an hour moving debris until we found stairs to the surface.

We stood under the turbulent Terran sky with the ruins of London spread at our feet. The city that had survived two world wars looked like a petulant giant had smashed all his toys and left the mess. A cool wind blew rock dust into devils that broke apart against our legs.

I turned into the setting sun—oh, how a real sun felt good on my tired face!—and spotted a pile of gray-white stone that could have been Buckingham Palace. Letting out my keening, I searched for life among the rubble. I should have sensed a few hearty survivors who'd bet that no bombs would fall on a city already reduced to ash. But either I was too exhausted from our weeks on the road or London was a true desolation.

Timberfoot's hand snaked into mine.

I still didn't have the measure of the man. At times, his magic seemed too big to be contained by his broad-shouldered frame. But he could also reel it in and wrap it tightly inside himself so that no whiff of power remained. It was a fantastic trick, one that I'd secretly been trying to copy during the long nights on the road. But sometimes, like now, his magic sang of sorrow. Like me, he felt the senseless destruction of two worlds in his very bones.

"Are we doing the right thing?" I asked. "Maybe there's no point in closing the doors." *Maybe there's no one left to protect from the demon.*

Timberfoot squinted into the setting sun. His eyes crinkled at the edges, and I wondered if he'd once had reason to laugh often.

"People are out there. When we're done in Underhill, we'll go find them."

I squeezed his hand, trying to fill that gesture with all my gratitude. My self-imposed mission hadn't made his life easier, but still he followed me.

"Scouts say that trolls are on the horizon!" Gander shouted through the door. "We go now!"

We dashed back into the bright, unending summer day of Underhill.

At each door, Gander took longer and longer to ready himself. This time, I found him stepping into an odd silver box set up beside the gate's generator. Copper rods protruded from each corner and bent at forty-five degree angles, with needle-like tips pointing inward.

"It's an amplifier." The dwarf pulled on his beard. His gaze slid away from mine. "I...uh, don't have enough left in me to spark the blade, you see."

"I understand." Gander had been the one to teach me about magic amplifiers. "Will it be enough?"

"Should be. Let's have a go." He stepped into the box and anchored the first three needles into his stomach and hips, cursing at each bite. "Help me with that last one." I gripped the rod and pressed it against the fleshy part of his rump. "Don't be shy about it."

I clenched my teeth, crushed my compassion, and drove the needle into his butt.

"Lugh's teats! You don't need to split my gizzard in two!"

My hands fluttered uselessly at the rods. I wanted to help and didn't know how. Gander brushed me away and turned his attention inward.

His right hand gripped his sword while his left cradled the bloated umbilical cord that linked the ley-line to the portal.

"Sword" was an ambitious name for Gander's blade. At twelve inches, it was more of a knife, though it looked bigger in the dwarf's small hands. But it had presence, a weight that came with any weapon forged in the dwarven mines at Brhim Toldur. My fingers still itched to hold it.

The cord's magic hummed and sizzled, filling the air with a hot-sour-fizzy taste. But soon I keened another source of power. Gander primed the blade from his own well, his magic intensified by the silver box. The power sharpened and grew until it felt like bugs skittering over my skin.

When I could stand it no longer—when I thought my seams might split—Gander released his pent up magic. The blade clanged against the cord like the clapper of a great bell. The backlash reverberated through my joints.

But the cord held.

Gander slashed again. Beads of sweat lit his face.

He was pouring all of his magic into it. He would have nothing left. A body without magic was just a corpse.

I lurched forward to stop him, but Timberfoot gripped my hand. I shook off the dryad and seized Gander's shoulder. I fed him everything I had.

Magic bloomed.

Gander's head shot back. His eyes rolled to white. His sword severed the cord like it was a blade of grass.

London Door slammed shut.

I crumpled into Timberfoot's arms. My stomach gnawed on my backbone. The sky was too bright, the air too thin, the silence too full of echoes.

Gander plucked the needles from his skin and rounded on me.

"Of all the stupidities! You could have died!" He saw my shaking hands pressed against my chest, and his tone softened. "I taught you better, lass. Don't ever try such a thing again!"

I nodded. My tongue was a thick mass in my mouth.

"Swear it!"

"I swear."

But we had two more doors to close. Only divine intervention would let me keep that oath.

Nunavut Door

Over the winter and spring, Gander, Timberfoot and I traveled to the remotest parts of Underhill. We closed every door but two. At each one, the garrison commanders gave me sealed messages from the King's Council. I recognized Eamon's elegant hand, and I had no illusions about who was in charge back at the Winter Palace. The first letter demanded that I stand down, abandon my foolish quest, and take my rightful place at court. The next called me a traitor to my people, a monster for abandoning my family. A human-lover.

The last packet, handed to me by an old wounded sergeant at London Door, was a heavy weight in my pocket. Along with Eamon's usual harangue, there was another letter sealed with the queen's signet. Mother dropped all formalities and begged me to be safe. She had given up trying to convince the Council to evacuate. Anyone who wanted to leave had already done so. But Winter City was still stuffed to bursting with refugees and soldiers from far-flung garrisons. And Horak's army was set up on the plains outside the gates. The city was under siege.

As we road across the northern desert toward Nunavut Door, I pulled out the letter. The page was smudged with dirt because I'd read it a dozen times. I poured over her lines again, wishing they said more. Her last words were:

"If nothing else, we will stand firm against the demon's forces. I only hope our sacrifice will give you the time you need. Do not listen to the Council, my daughter. Do what must be done and don't worry about us. Your father and I are exactly where we need to be. But you must go on. Live to be the queen I know you can be."

The words blurred as I read them again. It took all my will not to turn my horse for home.

"You're still worrying about your family," Timberfoot said.

"How can I not?" My parents wouldn't leave the castle until Horak took it from them. And then it would be too late.

He nodded, looking over my head at some other horizon. "The wind will blow and the leaves will fall."

"Don't give me any of your dryad platitudes. I'm not in the mood."

Timberfoot grinned and kicked his mount. "A race, then."

After months on the road, he looked only slightly less uncomfortable on horseback. No matter how we adjusted the stirrups, his legs were too long, so he now rode bareback on a sturdy plow horse we'd found abandoned.

I rode a sorrel mare I'd commissioned from the garrison at London Door. She wasn't as fleet or as graceful as Segrid, but after months of being cooped up, she was eager to run.

"Don't think you can beat me, do you?"

Timberfoot's beard only partially hid his grin. "Nope. But it will be a pleasure to see you ride away."

Heat rushed up my face. I covered the glow his words sparked in me by kicking the mare into a canter. Timberfoot's old plow horse snorted once and tried to match our speed.

Gander swore behind me as his pony broke into a trot. I felt only a moment of guilt for leaving him behind before the joy of galloping down an empty forest lane seized me. The wind howled a war cry in my ears. The sorrel and I ran until the lines between woman and horse blurred, ran until joy filled my lungs, ran until…

A man hung on a signpost.

The mare shot past the crossroads. I hauled on her reins, and she swung her neck around, eyes showing white.

"Easy." I turned her in circles until she calmed and then walked her over to examine the corpse hanging on the crossroads sign.

His eyes were nothing but black holes. Skin flaked from his desiccated face and a shock of white hair blew around his head like milkweed fluff. This man had died to feed Horak.

We'd seen the destruction of his army before, seen the dried out husks left behind in the hundreds, victims of Horak's thirst for magic. But this felt personal.

Timberfoot finally caught up, his eyes shining with glee from our race until they fell on the signpost.

"A message," he said.

"Yes."

Horak was taunting us. *Whatever road you take, I will find you,* his message said.

It also told me that he was getting worried. With only two doors left to close, Horak felt the cage closing around him.

The hanging man gave me no clues to how long he'd been dead. It could have been hours or weeks. I scanned the road and in all directions, looking for that telltale haze of dust signaling an army on the march.

The next door was still a day's ride ahead. I wouldn't sleep until I saw Gander cut its cord.

A SPIDER TROLL hit my wrist, sending a shock wave up my arm. I dropped my knife, dove for an abandoned sword. Gravel scored my fingers as I grabbed the hilt. No time for pain. I whirled and slashed down, severing a head. Ocher blood burst from the wound, splattering my shirt and pants. No time for squeamishness. Turn. Slash. Kill. No time to count the bodies.

Horak's minions had been waiting for us. We broke through their line only because the soldiers from Nunavut garrison hadn't abandoned their post.

Now Timberfoot and I, along with the remaining soldiers, were arrayed around Nunavut Door, protecting Gander as he mustered his magic. The dryad had given into the inevitable and picked up a sword. A troll leapt at him. Timberfoot swung the blade like a bat, hurling the beast to a home run. He was grinning.

Slash. Kill. Turn.

Gander stood inside his amplifier, cursing as he strained to work the magic. Behind him, the icy fields of the Terran North shone like a beacon. We had to hold off the trolls until he succeeded.

To my right, a soldier screamed. I stumbled backward. My foot crushed something soft. An arm or a leg. No time for the bile rising in my throat.

Kill. Turn. Slash.

I keened a surge of power. The door slammed shut. Its echo shook my bones.

And suddenly the battle was over. The trolls skittered away into the forest. They had failed to stop us and now they would report to their god. I hoped they would pay for their failure.

The dead lay in heaps, spidery legs broken and tangled with fae and human limbs.

Timberfoot swept me up in one arm and kissed me. I breathed in his leafy scent, so much better than the sharp tang of blood in the air. He put me down and cupped my face, pressing his forehead against mine.

We're alive, his magic sang.

Only one door left.

I turned to congratulate Gander. The dwarf sagged over the side of his amplifier. Only the rods piercing his skin at cardinal points held him upright. His eyes were open and sightless.

My old tutor was dead.

AFTER WE BURIED Gander and burned the spiders, the soldiers packed up the garrison. As they were leaving, I pulled aside one young officer. He'd been promoted to Captain for one achievement. He was the most experienced soldier to have survived the fight.

"Come with us," I begged him. "King's Door is our last stop. Come through to Terra where you'll be safe." I felt like a snake oil salesman. We might make it to Terra, only to be met with bombs, mobs, disease or starvation. All the byproducts of war. But staying in Underhill meant utter annihilation. We lived in a time when shades of "certain death" mattered.

The soldier shook his head slowly. "We are the King's men. We'll stand by him."

"Horak will kill everyone in Winter City. He'll drink your magic until nothing is left but mummified skin stuck to splintering bones." There was no point in sugar coating it.

He opened his mouth to answer, then closed it and shook his head again.

The soldiers headed out the main gate, leaving us with provisions and their empty beds. I was grateful for both. After a hot meal, I fell onto a cot in the officer's quarters, convinced sleep would claim me at once. But the air in my room was humid and stale. The army issue blanket chaffed like nettles. I fidgeted on the cot. I fluffed the pancake pillow and forced my eyes to stay closed. It was no use.

I padded barefoot down the hall to the next room.

"Tim?"

"I'm here."

He was sitting up in his bunk. Light from one high window brushed his skin with gold. He'd shaved again, and he looked less like a mountain man. The camp blanket was snugged against his waist. Above that he wore nothing but a leather cord around his neck with a pendant nestled in the light fuzz of red hair on his chest.

"I don't want to be alone." My voice sounded small. I almost asked if we could talk. But that would be a lie. I didn't want to talk.

Timberfoot lifted his blanket and invited me to join him in his bed.

The Last Door

Timberfoot marched the road that led through Mab's Forest with his tree-trunk arms crossed over his chest.

"You cannot do this," he said.

"I can."

"Gander died closing the doors."

"Gander closed eight doors. I only need to close one."

My hand clutched the hilt of the dwarven knife that I'd coveted for so long. Its magic was cheeky. I kept thinking I heard children's nursery songs, but it was the sword thrumming in my hand. Its buoyant magic infected me, and I hummed along with it.

Timberfoot stopped and pulled me to face him.

"I don't want you to die." He filled his words with so much more than vowels and consonants.

"I'll be fine." I brushed him off and kept walking. I knew my chances of surviving the door-closing spell were slim, but the sword's magic filled me with optimism. I side-eyed the stalking dryad. By the rigid set of his shoulders, he didn't feel the same.

I'd left King's Door for last. It was a well-guarded secret. Camouflaged by powerful wards and hidden in Mab's Forest, no one but the King's inner circle knew it existed. Horak's minions had been waiting for us at the last door, but they'd have to trip over King's Door to find it.

I spotted movement ahead. My muscles tensed for a fight, and then some part of me recognized the proud stance of the soldier standing in the entrance to the cave that hid King's Door. My feet were running before my brain could catch up.

"Leighna!" Timberfoot yelled.

But I was already away, throwing my arms around my baby brother. Alvar squirmed as I kissed him on both cheeks.

"Enough!" He laughed. "You'll embarrass my honor guard." The soldiers lined up along the cave wall pretended not to hear. "Merry meet, sister."

"Merry meet, brother." I hugged him again. Alvar, the child of my heart, now grown into a man. He'd been only seventy-six when I left for Terra, barely a grown man by Duannan reckonings. And while he still had the round cheeks and complexion of a boy, his eyes were icy hard. Like me, he'd seen too much death in the last year.

"How did you know where to find me?" I asked.

"Mother said it only made sense that you'd leave King's Door for last in your mad quest."

"Mother? Is she here then? And Father?"

"No. They wouldn't come." His words faded as Timberfoot joined us.

"This is my brother, Alvar," I said.

"Good." Timberfoot smiled grimly. "Convince your sister to give up her suicidal plan." I'd become used to his looming presence and forgotten just how big he was. Next to Alvar's trim elegance, Timberfoot was a wild thing—tall, broad, raggedly bearded. Menacing.

Alvar eyed him up and down, his mouth pinched thin. I knew he was assessing the dryad and found him lacking in courtly manners. My brother was a snob, just as I had been before living a simple life on Terra.

Alvar took a step back. "Actually, I come with a message from the Council. They told me to tell you…you were right. Close the doors at any cost. And soon."

My heart shuddered like a lantern in a storm. The Winter Court was making a last stand then. I took no satisfaction in being right.

We had no time for a family reunion. If Horak was at the palace, he would soon torture the whereabouts of King's Door from some poor advisor.

I stepped through the door, expecting to find a deserted park in a Pennsylvania suburb, and stopped short at the sight before me.

Hundreds, possibly thousands of people sat cross-legged among Iona Park's standing stones. They were dirty and half-clothed, with the feral look of spirits who might suddenly spook and disappear into the forest. Gasps rippled through the crowd upon our arrival. Even the most talented human couldn't have spotted the warded door from this side, and so it seemed like we appeared from mid-air.

A circle of standing stones loomed out of the darkness like silent sentinels in the dim light. A bonfire burned high in the middle of this circle and children dashed around unchecked. Most of them wore rags or went naked in the summer heat. And everything—the ground, the air, the standing stones at my back—sizzled with magic.

Iona Park was a car-ride from great cities like New York and Philadelphia and was only built in the last century. The standing stones might look out of place in an American suburb, but this tiny patch of land had been sacred long before the park's installation. It was a junction point, a site where ley-lines crossed. Someone had labored to set up these stones in the 1970s, mimicking the Celtic henges of the old world—someone who'd recognized the power lines that intersected here.

"This is a sacred place," Timberfoot whispered. "Be wary. These people might not welcome your intrusion."

I nodded. I'd seen gatherings like this in Arizona. Sanctuaries where humans waited out bombs and prayed for their gods to save them. I made a split-second decision to use their awe for good.

"Citizens of Terra!" I infused my voice with power so that every soul in the park could hear me as if I spoke the words for their ears only. "I am Queen Leighna of the Duannae." The truth of those words tasted like ash. I was only queen because my mother, a greater queen than I could ever aspire to be, was lost.

I slashed the door with Gander's sword, breaking the ward that concealed it. Pennsylvania was still dark, the sky only hinting at dawn, but Underhill shone bright blue and green through the shimmering gate. The humans were on their feet now.

"This is Underhill. My home that is being ravaged by a demon set loose first on your world. You might not know the hunger of a true demon." By the expressions of the crowd, I could see that these people had lived through enough horrors. They could imagine a lot. "But he will come for you, just as he came for my people." Murmurs rippled through the crowd. I spoke over them. "For a year, I rode through Underhill destroying every door to Terra. This door is the last. I don't know that I have the skill to close it. But I will try.

Will you lend me the power of your prayers? Will you help me trap Horak, so he never destroys another world?"

The humans were silent. One woman with tangled white hair and a face lined with wisdom approached. She laid a crown of yellow flowers on my head and smiled.

"Be welcome here, Leighna, Queen of the fae. On this day of Litha, the power of Sullis and Lugh are yours."

Litha. It was midsummer. Had a year passed already, since I fled Tucson? On this day—the heart of the summer—ley-lines would be pregnant with power. Maybe…just maybe, I could pull this off.

I PRESSED MY palms against an upright foundation stone and keened power surging through the spaces between its atoms. This would do. I cleared away last winter's debris of leaves and sticks and sat, pressing the backs of my thighs against bare earth. I wished for Gander's poise, or at least his amplifier, but we'd left the gadget behind. It had burned out taking the dwarf's life, and I had no alchemical knowledge to fix it. But I had his blade and his years of teaching. It would have to be enough.

Timberfoot crouched beside me, filling my space with his bulk.

"I cannot persuade you away from this folly?"

Just stand by me, I wanted to say. *If I live through this, I will let you persuade me to anything.*

"No."

"Then take this." He pulled off the thong at his neck and dropped its medallion in my palm. It was a tree of life, carved in jade. He closed my fingers around it. "For luck."

I tied the leather strands around my neck and let the medallion hang between my breasts where it sat, heavy and hot and full of unfulfilled promise.

"I'll make it through. I'll close the damned door and then…" My throat was thick with tears.

His hands cupped my chin, kissed me. "And then anything is possible."

I let myself fall into his ivy-green eyes. But only for a moment. There was work to do.

Timberfoot went to stand beside Alvar. His hulking presence seemed as formidable as the standing stones. I pushed down the regret burning through me like an ulcer and began the long descent into stillness, searching for the raw power of the ley-lines.

The portal's cord, pulled through from the other side, lay across my lap. It pulsed with gathering potential, a snake lying in wait to ambush its prey. I would kill that snake. And this time, when the door shut, I'd be forever trapped on the Terran side.

I gripped Gander's knife with icy fingers. It hummed one of its pretty little ditties. For so long, I had coveted this blade, and now I only wished for Gander back, so he could wield it instead of me.

The humans raised their voices in another song, amplifying the magic of this sacred space. It filled me, boosting my own paltry magic. But my mind raced, and I could find no way to calm it. Images of my parents fighting off an army of spiders kept invading my thoughts. I saw the white spires of the Winter Palace crumble under the demon's fist. Sweat drenched my hair and my collar. I opened my eyes and spied Alvar conferring with Timberfoot. What could those two have to say to each other?

No.

I had to block them out, erase fear for my family, my longings, and my exhaustion. There could only be me and the spell. I ran my hands along the distended cord. A flash of Horak's army raging toward the last door filled my vision for an instant. I ruthlessly pushed it aside.

Just me and the spell.

I breathed deeply and began again. Magic flowed from the ley-line. It felt glorious as it shivered through me, glorious like the meaning in the ancient tongue—bringing joy and wonder. The humans raised their voices as one, adding power of prayer to the mix. Magic sizzled along my skin to the knife in my hand.

I could do this. I was ready. I tucked the blade under the cord. One sharp tug upward and I would sever two worlds forever. There would be no going home.

My hands ached on the knife's grip. Magic surged through me, as mercurial as a rapture. It filled me to the bursting point.

And in that moment, I knew I'd failed.

It was too much! Panic clawed at my throat. Timberfoot was right. I would never survive this spell. But it was so much worse than that. I was caught in a maelstrom—power from the ley-line, the human prayers, the blade. It would crack me into a million shards and scatter me across the universe.

Rough hands jolted me out of my trance, clamping my arms behind me, and hauling me upright. I dropped the knife. The world spun. Magic fizzled away, taking a layer of my skin with it. I screamed, and a hand clamped over my mouth.

"Shh, sister. It's better this way." Alvar held me tightly. I struggled against the gag and he eased his grip. "Look." He pointed my face toward the door.

My heart jagged a beat, leaving a ragged hole in my chest.

Timberfoot stood with one foot in either world, cradling the cord in both hands. His chest expanded, and he threw back his head. Green light shot from his eyes. And with a primal roar, he tore the cord in two.

The door winked out. But Timberfoot wasn't done.

His legs twisted and he screamed as bones retooled themselves into roots. His right leg burrowed deep into Underhill. The left sank into soft Pennsylvania earth.

I thrashed in my brother's grip, trying to break free, wanting to stop this madness, but Alvar hung on. I could only watch in horror as Timberfoot's chest bucked and morphed, doubling in size, then tripling. Bark grew over his skin like a parasite—up his legs, stomach, neck…

When it reached his eyes, he turned them on me one last time and smiled.

And my world splintered.

Branches shot from his body. They sprouted great swaths of green leaves. And he grew. Oh, so impossibly high, until the canopy of his branches blocked the dawn.

In the sudden quiet, I could hear someone sobbing and realized it was me. I wrenched my arms from Alvar's grip. The humans had ended their song and gaped at the massive oak that had spawned in moments.

I laid my head against the trunk—too wide for my arms to circle—gripping the pendant he'd gifted me in one hand. I keened for the deep thrum of life inside.

There it was. Timberfoot's peculiar breezy magic.

My tears ran freely, feeding the soil where he'd rooted. I gripped his pendant in my hand and pounded his trunk until blood leaked through my fingers. Then I crumpled to the ground.

Around me, voices were raised in fear, anger, awe…it didn't matter. I would have died to close the door, but Timberfoot made sure I didn't have to. Had I worked my spell, my native land would have been lost to us forever, but I could keen the taste of Underhill in this great tree. Its roots pierced the veil so that one day, I might go home again. In the meantime, Horak would never get past the new guardian between worlds, Timberfoot Greenleaf.

On legs that could barely hold my weight, I left the little glade with its standing stones now dwarfed by the massive oak. My brother's voice ghosted after me. He was calling me back, but I ignored him. Alvar could follow or not. I didn't care.

I turned east as the sun rose. East toward the great human city, New York. I didn't know what I'd find there. It might be rubble, or it might be a haven for survivors. But whatever I found, I knew we could rebuild. We would survive.

Timberfoot Greenleaf had promised me anything was possible.

THE GIRL WHO CRIED BANSHEE

1

June 2070

Two steps into Abbott's Agora open air market, the scent of roasted meat and garlic siren-called to me. Color sprouted from hand-dyed fabrics. Fruit and vegetables laid on trestle tables smelled so vivid, I could taste them. The air buzzed with a dozen languages. And the magic suffusing everything? Well, that was neither smell nor sight, taste nor sound but a bastard blend of all these. A blend only someone with the keening power could sense.

Someone like me, Kyra Greene—exiled Valkyrie, failing entrepreneur, sucker for a furry face.

In my younger days, the Agora's magic would have overloaded my keening. A seizure wouldn't have been out of the question. But since returning to Montreal—with all the post-war magic flying around like explosive shrapnel— I'd learned to ward myself against such an awful alchemic assault. I took a moment to reinforce that ward now, one psychic block at a time.

Breathe. Block. Breathe. Block.

Breeeathe. Breeeathe.

Learning to ward myself was the only magic my mother had given me— that and the two-and-a-half-foot long Valkyrie sword strapped to my back. But neither swords nor wards could defeat the lure of roasted souvlaki. And a few minutes later I found myself standing in front of the meat merchant's shack, drooling over a slowly turning lamb shank like a vampire at a blood drive.

I couldn't remember the last time I'd eaten meat.

"You buying?" The cook's pale aura fizzled. When I didn't answer, he held up one beautiful, blackened skewer of meat.

I wanted that meat.

I pulled out my widget and scrolled to my bank account.

Ouch.

Not even enough to cover my looming mortgage payment, and I still had to buy feed for my abaia eel and an injured ice sprite. Souvlaki was a luxury I couldn't afford. But hunger prowled in my gut, sharpened its claws on my resolve, and I tapped my widget to the merchant's, making the payment.

"Thanks." I wandered along the cracked pavement path, nibbling my meat hoard. Maybe if I took longer to eat it, my stomach would think it was a full meal.

If my pest control business made money, I could buy plenty of food. But so far, that hadn't panned out. Maybe my Sayntanne neighborhood was too far outside the city. Maybe I needed to advertise more. Maybe I'd overestimated the rampancy of fae infestations. Whatever the problem, I needed to cut costs. That meant hardening my resolve and finding homes for some of my rescues. Which was the mission behind today's trip.

I finished my treat and tossed the skewer in a recycler. Shouts came from ahead, and two Viking-wannabes pitched out of a beer garden, punching and cursing. A bottle of beer smashed on the road, filling the air with the smell of hops. Their scuffling knocked me off my feet, and I landed hard, scraping my palms on pavement.

My sword, sensing a battle, squeed in its sheath.

The men—one red-headed and one dark—struggled to put each other in headlocks. They weren't really fighting. I'd known enough true Vikings to recognize a brotherly brawl, but they punched hard enough to rattle bones. Red flipped the other one, restraining his arms and legs like tying a hog, and accidentally pinning my leg too. I squirmed to free it and he glanced up, teeth bared in a feral grin. Our gazes locked. His eyes were Icelandic blue, his beard robin-breast red and…

…and suddenly I was transported back to my grandfather's hall in Asgard. My Aesir cousins were brawling over spilled mead. Aunt Dana watched with a pained but patient frown. And Aaric was kissing and tickling and teasing me—always teasing me.

My heart lurched.

I closed my eyes and opened them again, forcing my brain to see what was in front of me. By the One-eyed Father, they were just a couple of guys. Human guys. I had to stop seeing Aaric in every face in the crowd.

Aaric was dead. Dead by my hand and no combination of wish-regret-denial would change that.

My stomach churned with garlic and guilt, but I'd get over it. I always did. And those episodes of seeing Aaric's hands, his eyes, his crooked mouth with its little griffin-got-the-canary grin—if they weren't fading, at least they were less frequent.

I kicked out hard and Red grunted. Good. I stood, dusted gravel off my hands and headed for the far end of the market where I'd find Nesi Wares, a shop that specialized in feed for uncommon creatures.

The cobbled path took a hairpin turn into Obfuscation Alley. I strolled past a different class of vendors—purveyors of potions and tinctures, relics and magical talismans (some with real power) and all manner of arcane goods and services. But when I reached the corner where I expected to find Nesi, his shop was gone. In its place was a canopy over a table of dried chicken heads and voodoo fetches.

"What happened to Nesi's?" I asked the crone behind the table.

"Nothin'. Shop's over there." She pointed across the road and three stalls down.

Huh. I could have sworn his shop had been on this corner last week.

The old woman grinned, showing off her one remaining tooth.

"The market's alive, girl. Don't blink or you'll find yourself on a different road altogether." Her words wormed around my ward like a prophecy sniffing for a way inside.

I nodded and headed over to Nesi's, pushing aside the ratty canvas he used as a door in warm weather.

Nesi was busy cleaning a bird cage. A crow-ish bird with purple feet stood on his shoulder. A dozen cages hung from the ceiling. These held more exotic birds with brilliant plumage, lizard tails or spear-sharp horns—all curiosities that would fetch a good price. Aquariums and terrariums lined one wall. Along another wall, shelves were stacked high with bags of feed and supplies that you would never get at your local Pet Mart.

Nesi found me a few months back when he answered my ad to re-home a venomous pixie viper. I was hesitant to hand over the snake at first, but some snooping proved that Nesi was on the up and up. He sold only to real collectors, not health and fitness mongers or dark magic practitioners who would gut a beast for its blood, bones and bile.

On the few occasions that I could bring myself to part with a fae critter, I gave Nesi first dibs.

He looked up from his dirty work and smiled. His left eye was clear as iced vodka. His right was cloudy as curdled milk—and it leaked down his cheek. Looking at it made me uncomfortable. Living with it had to be worse. Nesi survived the Flood Wars. And like most veterans, he didn't talk about it.

"Kyra Greene, Princess of the Pleiades!" He wiped his hands on his grimy apron. "What brings you here this fine morning?"

Just to be clear, I'm not a princess, not of a distant star cluster, not of a fae or human court. Not of any dominion in this world or another.

Nesi had strange ideas that were best left unexplored or you risked opening yourself to one of his mega-watt rants. He could sound off for hours about Pluto falling out of planetary favor or the carcinogenic effects of the ward that protected all of Montreal like an invisible and impenetrable bubble. And never, never get him talking about "them" and the mysterious aliens "they" were always protecting. In all these months I still hadn't figured out who "they" were. I wasn't sure Nesi knew.

Today, his shirt was on the right way round. His yellow-gray hair looked almost neat, and his magic hummed along at a steady pitch. Those were good signs. Lucid signs.

"I brought you this." I held up a jar. Inside was a green and purple iridescent beetle.

Nesi raised it to the dim gleam floating just below the ceiling and squinted at the bug.

"Pretty, but what's so unusual about it?"

"May I?" I pointed to a half-eaten bagel on the counter. He nodded. I opened the jar, dropped in a few crumbs and locked the lid back in place. The beetle devoured the crumbs then belched out a flame that licked around the inside of the jar.

"Splendid!" Nesi's one good eye lit up as bright as the beetle's flame. "You should really start a blog about your marvelous creatures."

"I don't have time for that."

"Of course, of course. It was just a thought." He flipped through his super-secret critter catalogue on his widget. "Let's see now. Ah! Here it is. Combustion beetle. A decent find. I'll give you a hundred for it."

A hundred bucks would fill my cupboard with rice and oatmeal for a month.

"A hundred and fifty." Nesi wouldn't respect me if I didn't haggle. "And you have to assure me it goes to a true collector, not someone who'll grind it into beetle dust."

"A hundred and fifteen. And you know I can only guarantee the first buyer. I'll make sure it goes to a good home. But after that?" He shrugged and his cloudy eye twitched and dripped.

"A hundred and twenty."

"If you're so worried, you could just drop it off in the Inbetween yourself." His good eye slitted like he was looking down the barrel of a rifle, and a mean little smile twisted his lips. "Or are you afraid, Princess?"

"I'm not a Princess!" I balled a fist and pounded the counter. The bird on Nesi's shoulder squawked and ruffled his wings. I smoothed my own ruffled feathers. "Just because I won't go into the wilds alone, doesn't mean I'm afraid." Only three types of people ventured outside the wards—homesteaders, marauders and vampires.

"Hey, no offense." Nesi held up his hands in surrender. "That's not why I called you Princess."

"I know." I slumped on the stool beside the counter. Nesi took my beetle and tapped his widget to mine to transfer the money.

His good eye sized me up. "It's your aura, you know. I've only seen one like it, on a princess…"

"…from a water planet in the Pleiades cluster. You told me." Every time I visited he told me about my otherworldly aura. "And this woman—she told you she was an alien princess?"

"Of course not." Nesi tapped the side of his nose. "They told me. They're always listening. Always watching and whispering. Yak, yak, yak." He squeezed his thumb and fingers together to puppet the sound.

"Right."

"Did you need anything else today?" He limped behind the counter piled high with books and semi-precious stones.

"Just some crayfish for my eel, please. And do you have any idea what an ice sprite eats?"

Nesi dropped two dozen tiny crustaceans in a canvas sack, then plucked another pouch from the shelf. "Try this. It's ground pine cone mixed with a few minerals."

I held out my widget for payment, but Nesi waved it away.

"Consider it a bonus for the beetle. You should have haggled better."

Damn. I knew I could have gone higher.

"And you know, if you weren't so worried about going into the Inbetween, I'd have a job for you."

"What do you mean?"

"I get homesteaders in here from time to time, when they get visas to enter the ward. There's a rare infestation of some critter east of here. A fishing village called Ors, along the river. Their elders sent a request for help. They'll pay decent money to clear the infestation. That's what you do, isn't it?"

Yep, that was me. Valkyrie Pest Control. But did I really want to go outside the ward, where the only rule of law was whoever had the strongest weapons and magic?

"What kind of infestation?"

"Don't know. Grub or vermin. Does it matter? Pays good. Four thousand. Higher fee for hazard pay."

Four thousand! Today's boost from the beetle would feed me for a month, but after that? My truck needed work, my computer was on life-support, and I couldn't remember the last time I used real shampoo in my hair.

"You interested?" He watched me with his steady, lopsided gaze.

"Maybe."

Was I seriously considering a trip to the Inbetween? People died in the Inbetween, died in horrible, gruesome ways. Beheading? Sure the Inbetween had a monster for that. Desanguination? Check. Vampires for that. Intestines liquefying through your belly-button? The Inbetween could find a magical mutant mosquito to inflict that pain-party on you.

But my cupboards held one bag of rice and a few withered yams. And there were the mortgage gods to appease.

"How long to get there?" I looked up to find Nesi watching me. "I mean it. How long's the trip?"

"A few hours. They'll send a boat. Someone will pick you up in Barrows."

I considered it for only a moment longer. Any more and I would have lily-livered out.

"Tell them I won't take less than five thousand. And that might go up after I assess the situation."

"I'm sure that's reasonable." Nesi's grin was half mocking and half reassuring.

Three days later, I left the haven of Montreal Ward to meet my guide in Barrows.

Barrows spread away from Montreal's north gate with ill-conceived streets that twisted and dead-ended for no reason. A few merchants plied their wares along the road to the gate, but inns took up most of the real-estate—way stations for travelers hoping to get visas onto the island. There were a good number of pubs too, catering to homesteader farmers who bought day passes to sell their produce in the city markets.

My guide was supposed to meet me at a pub called The Hook and Tackle. Even though we were nowhere near the sea, a waft of brine hit me when I opened the tavern's door. A dozen scarred tables were huddled around a hearth that was bare and dark in the June heat.

I'd arrived before the lunch crowd, and only one patron sat slumped over a mug of ale. A round-faced woman with splotchy cheeks dried dishes behind the bar. She watched me with unguarded curiosity as I approached.

"I'm looking for Liam Geary."

"He ain't here."

"Then I'll wait."

"This ain't a library. Nothing is free. Not even waitin'."

I ordered beer and paid her from the few copper coins I had in my pocket. Widgets worked this close to the ward, but the preferred currency in Barrows was cash or trade rather than electronic transfers. The barkeep set a glass of warm beer before me. I took a sip and tried not to wince. It was flat as old leather.

During the next hour, a dozen people wandered in for lunches of stew and bread or just a cup of ale. I nursed my drink, not wanting to waste more coins. My foot bounced on the rung of the barstool.

What was I doing here? Already, leaving the safety of the ward seemed like a colossally bad idea.

The Inbetween was a dangerous place. Pockets of magic could open under your feet like quicksand. The weather was unpredictable, followed no true seasons, and could change from one moment to the next. And the lush forests were filled with vampires, marauders and beasts of all sizes. At least that's what the stories said.

I hadn't been outside the ward since my trip home from Asgard. And then I enjoyed the security of a dryad escort to Manhattan Ward. From there, I hopped a ship that sailed right to Old Port in Montreal. I never got to enjoy the dangerous splendors of the Inbetween. I only half-believed the stories, but half was still enough to keep me inside the city gates. Until now.

Maybe this wasn't such a great idea. And this Liam guy wasn't going to show. I pushed away my glass and rose to leave.

"Kyra Greene?"

I turned to find a pair of dark brown eyes sizing me up. Eyes framed by a young but rugged face and a mop of bronze, sun-kissed curls.

"I'm Liam." He held out his hand. I shook it. Calloused fingers rasped against mine. His smile bent his lips downward in a way that usually meant smugness or arrogance. But Liam's eyes sparkled with friendly amusement.

"You're late." My tone was harsher than I intended, but it covered the little flutter in my chest. Liam was gorgeous.

The sharp tug of desire inside me was as surprising as his looks. I hadn't felt anything like it since…not since Aaric. He'd had that same downward-dog smile. I shied away from those thoughts and glowered at Liam to hide my discomfort.

"Navigating the river's always tricky." He dropped a coin on the bar and nodded for the barkeep to serve him a glass. "Came across a pod of sea serpents and they decided to have a little fun with me."

"Sea serpents?"

Liam laughed. "Don't look so green. You're not afraid of a few serpents, are you?"

I shook my head. He gulped down his beer and wiped the foam off his lip with the back of his hand.

"Well good, then. Let's head out. The trip back should be easier. We'll be heading downstream. Can I carry your bag?"

"No, thanks." I could carry my bag. He was a customer. I would do well to remember that. His gaze slid to my sword, then back to my face, which was quickly heating with a flush.

He smiled. "This way then."

Outside, the day had turned cool. Black clouds churned overhead. A church rang the noon bell. I felt every clang like a death sentence as we headed away from the city, away from civilization and safety.

"Is this your first time in the real world?" Liam asked.

"I wouldn't put it like that, but yes. More or less."

"A virgin!" He clapped his hands together. "I'll have to show you the sights proper then."

On the east end of town, the foot and cart traffic thinned. Liam acted the tour guide, pointing out every rock and shrub.

"See those trees over there? Chestnut. It's a popular rest spot in the fall when the nuts are ripe. Free food is always good food. And that there is a mule cart. We use them for transport. Did you just roll your eyes at me?"

"I know what a mule cart is. I'm from the city, not Mars."

"I'm just jazzing you. That's how you wardies talk, right? Jazzing you?"

I rolled my eyes again. "Whatever."

He whistled as we strode out of town. Even the spitting rain didn't dampen his spirits.

"Is it safe to sail in this weather?" I inspected the darkening clouds.

"Technically, we won't be sailing. More like a gentle float downstream."

He grinned again and despite my pique, I felt that traitorous tug of desire.

"So you're one of those," I said.

"One of what?"

"One of those people who corrects others for no reason, other than to feel superior."

He laughed.

"I like you Kyra Greene. I think we'll get along just fine."

The wind surged, whirling up a funnel of leaves into our path. Debris caught in the whirlwind, twisting, writhing, and morphing into the clear image of a flower. Then a star. Then a face.

"Watch it!" Liam grabbed my hand and yanked me sideways as the little cyclone blustered by.

"What was that?"

"Leaf devil. It's a portal, sort of. Step into it and you'll end up who-knows-where. I know a boy who stepped through a devil and ended up down south, past Manhattan Ward. Took him three years to get home."

It seemed an unlikely story, but I watched the leaf devil until it swirled into a bush and broke apart. After that, my eyes never stopped roaming the shadows on either side of the road. When thunder pealed, I jumped and Liam laughed, like I'd done something funny.

"Relax, wardie. We're almost there."

A half-hour later, we turned off the road onto a narrow cart path. The storm had blown itself out and sunlight cut through the leaf cover. Liam continued to point out every conifer, bird and forest critter we encountered.

"And those are flying rats. Duck!"

A flock of gray creatures dive-bombed us from the trees. My first instinct was to go for my sword, and it trilled with glee in its sheath. Instead, I grabbed my hunting knife and slashed at a rat as it screeched by me. The thing was as big as a cat, with eyes like sunken raisins and inch-long fangs. The flock seethed around us, leathery gray wings blocking out the sunlight. My hand was slick with blood by the time the swarm flapped away like a great gray murmuration. Six gray bodies twitched at my feet.

"Were you bitten?" Liam asked. His hair was messed over his forehead, and a streak of blood cut across his face. He was still grinning. Did nothing faze this guy?

"N…no I don't think so." I inspected my hand, knuckles still clasping the knife like a lifeline. "No. I'm okay."

"Good. Then take a deep breath. That was just the opening act. This forest hides things worse than rats, winged or not."

Blood pounded at my temples. He squeezed my shoulder.

"Don't worry. You did well. And we're almost at the boat. Then we only have to worry about sea monsters."

"Terrific."

I wiped my blade on my handkerchief and was still trying to re-sheathe my knife when a rock exploded next to my foot. My mind registered the sound of gunfire a second later.

I turned to see a cabin, hidden in the trees. The muzzle of a shotgun poked through the cracked open door. Liam held up his hands in surrender.

"Just me, Mrs. Tensel," he called out.

"Someone lives here?" I whispered. Bad enough to live outside the ward, but all alone like that? I shivered just thinking of the things that could wander out of the forest to sample the crunchy creatures in the log cabin.

"Just old man Tensel and his wife. He lets people tie up at his dock for a fee. The old lady doesn't see too well anymore."

Somehow, the fact that our assailant's poor aim was due to blindness didn't make me feel better.

The door opened and a short, weathered woman stepped onto the porch.

"Ah, Liam, you're back." She bared blackened teeth and cradled the shotgun in her arms. "I didn't expect you so soon. You'll be staying for supper, then?"

"No, thank you, ma'am. I must get my precious cargo home before dark." He touched my shoulder. The woman pursed her lips and squinted, as if trying to take my measure.

"Well, take care, then. The winds are changeable today. And say hello to your auntie."

"I will."

Liam whistled as he headed down to the dock. I was starting to wonder if he was a psychopath or just unreasonably happy. It could be so hard to tell the difference.

3

The boat bobbing against the dock was no longer than four meters and half as wide. It was made of weathered wood that might have been painted blue in another life. Ropes looped around a single mast with a gray-white sail tucked around the boom. Standing in the middle of the deck, Liam could easily reach the oars locked onto either edge of the boat.

"You expect me to sail in that?"

His eyebrows shot up, and he laid a hand over his heart.

"You insult my boat, you insult me, my ancestors and my dog."

I looked around for the dog and Liam shrugged.

"Okay, no dog. It's bad luck to keep them near fishing tackle. But seriously, my father built this boat by hand, forty years ago. Today won't be the day it goes under, I promise."

He held out a hand, inviting me on board. I reached for him, and he wrapped an arm around my waist, picking me up in one smooth motion and dropping me onto the boat deck. He held on for a second longer than was necessary.

I pushed away, flashing him my best not-a-chance smile. He tipped his head with a guy's-gotta-try grin.

The rocking boat was already making me queasy, and I sat on the first thing I found—a wooden box at the back end of the deck. The stern, I thought, trying to remember my bits of nautical knowledge. I dropped my backpack at my feet like a barricade.

"Anyway, I said we won't be sailing. I've got a full tank of gas. We're cruising, baby!" His eyes were bright, and I had to laugh. He knew he was charming, and he knew just how to use that charm to his advantage.

"I need to get into that locker or we won't be going far." Liam took my bag and tossed it toward the front—the bow. I stood and tried to step past him. The boat rocked and pitched. A squeal escaped from my lungs. I squeezed my eyes shut, then opened them to find Liam grinning at me. He plucked my fingers off his arm where I'd latched on tight enough to leave a mark and shuffled me backwards until my back hit the mast.

"Just wait here, wardie. I'll set the engine."

I ground my teeth to keep from throwing his insult back in his face. I didn't like being called wardie any more than I liked princess.

He's the customer, I kept reminding myself. Play nice. Besides, I was starting to understand that any quip I threw at Liam would be tossed back threefold. So I sat on the bench tucked up against the mast and watched him work.

He unlocked the box and hauled out a battered portable outboard engine.

"Can't be too careful out here," he said. "Even old lady Tensel's shotgun wouldn't keep a thief away from an outboard engine. They're worth their weight in gold."

In minutes, he had the motor clamped to the back of the boat and filled with gasoline. Then he pulled a worn board from the bottom of the locker and fitted it into a wedge beside the motor. He attached a tiller to that.

"That's seriously old school," I said. "I haven't seen a combustion engine in years."

Liam patted the motor. "Fifteen horsepower, electric start. She's a beauty. And almost a hundred years old, but still purrs like a kitten."

"And it runs on gas? Where do you get that?"

"You really are a wardie."

I scowled, but that only made his grin wider.

"We scavenge when we're not fishing. There are still a lot of resources out there." He pointed into the trees and the vast Inbetween. "And once in a while, if we're really good," he winked, "Terra spits out a bulla for us to plunder."

I'd heard the term "bulla" before. After the Flood Wars, when magic washed over the land, forests reclaimed much of civilization. Trees and dense underbrush grew over towns in months. Farm land disappeared even faster. And unless protected by a ward, cities rotted away and sank underground. It was no wonder many people adopted a belief in Terra, a sentient planet fighting back for herself after thousands of years of human bondage.

But once in a while, Terra gave back. A bulla was an eruption of the past. Sometimes it was a pre-war house that the earth vomited forth, wholly intact. Sometimes it was a factory or a school. I'd even heard of entire villages popping up like time-capsules from a lost era. Bullas were highly sought after prizes for scavengers who stripped them of metals and all other materials that could no longer be mined or manufactured in the post-war world.

"Do you really have bullas out here? I'd love to see one." I regretted the words as soon as they came out. I wasn't here to sight-see. Why did he make it so hard for me to remain professional?

"We'll have to see what we can do about that." His gaze rested on me like a soft caress. Then he seemed to remember himself and he turned back to the engine. In a moment he had it started and we pulled away from the dock.

THE AFTERNOON SUN felt good on my face and the breeze coming off the water wasn't too chilly. If only I didn't have to worry about sea serpents and marauders on shore, I might have enjoyed the journey.

"Your father really built this?" I asked.

"Yep. Mostly out of scraps of other boats. Our village pooled resources for the engine. We fish as a team, so it was an investment for them." While he spoke, he never stopped scanning the river and the forested shoreline.

"And did it pay off?" I asked, just to keep talking. His constant vigilance made me nervous.

"It did. But those were better times." The light in his eyes shaded like a cloud covering the sun. For once, he didn't seem inclined to say more. I changed the subject.

"How long until we get there?"

"If we make good time, we should be home before dark. You don't want to be out on the water after dark."

"You're doing it again."

"What's that?"

"Trying to scare me."

"Is it working?"

"Little bit."

Liam spent the next two hours sitting on the locker, one hand on the tiller, eyes always scouring ahead. I spent that time trying not to watch him. The wind blew his curls away from his face and he looked young. Too young for the thoughts that came to my mind.

I turned my attention to the shore whipping by. It was nothing but rich forest—no structures, no roads. The trees were massive, covered in vines and choked with underbrush. Once I saw the trees shake as if something huge was moving through them, but Liam gunned the engine and we were long gone by the time that something made it to water.

I shivered and wrapped my keening tightly around me, not wanting to sense the magic things out there.

When the river widened enough to be considered a lake, Liam kept our boat idling along the south shore.

"Shouldn't we see the village by now?" I asked. It was the grown-up version of "Are we there yet? How much longer?" Each kilometer we cruised away from Montreal, my nerves tightened a bit more. Everything felt so alien—the jungle-like forest, the briny air…the handsome man sitting close enough to touch.

"Just wait." He cut the engine back, and we drifted along with the current. Jagged slabs of rock jutted from the water ahead. Instead of steering around them, Liam edged us closer to shore. My hands pressed against my seat as I waited to hear the grinding shriek of the hull being torn open. But the boat found the only narrow lane through the rocks. Liam had clearly charted this route many times. He nudged the tiller left and right, squeezing the boat past the deadly obstructions.

Then we faced a wall of branches, brambles and vines. He put the boat in reverse, and we floated on the spot like a bee hovering over a flower.

"What's this?"

"Just wait." That seemed to be his favorite saying.

I didn't like being so close to the forest. Anything could pop out of the trees. We loitered there for a full minute before the wall of foliage swung toward us like a gate. Liam put the boat in gear and we cruised through the new gap. A teenaged girl waved to us from a wooden platform high in the trees. Liam waved back. I turned to watch the gate swing shut behind us. It would be nearly impossible for anyone to find that entrance. That meant it would be nearly impossible for anyone to find me. I shuddered and hugged my backpack to my chest. Not that anyone would come looking. I knew that when I took the job.

Here I am, alone in the wilds with a man I've never met. I was getting those psychopath vibes again. Why, oh why had I trusted Nesi's word?

I glanced at Liam in the dying light. He saw me looking and winked. Okay, so he didn't look like a serial killer. I took a deep breath and let out my keening to sense his magic again. Most people never knew when I was probing them this way, but Liam frowned and hunched his shoulders. Interesting. He had a touch of the keening himself but probably didn't know it.

In the old days, before magic broke the world, those with a sensitivity to the energies that fueled all life were given many names: witches, empaths, mediums and some less kindly labels. Now we might say he had an instinct for magic, but that didn't mean he understood the instinct.

I let my keening drop. It told me only that Liam was purely human and strangely content.

Serial killers could be content too.

I tried to pick out landmarks, but there were none. We floated down a canal built up on either side with stone walls. Past those, the trees were so tall and dense they met over the water like a peaked roof, blocking out most of the setting sun. If the village was at the end of this canal, raiders would have difficulty reaching it, even if they found the hidden gate. Guards could be posted in the trees on either side to rain down arrows and blaster fire.

"This is some set up you have."

Liam nodded. "Wards aren't the only way to protect yourself out here. Sometimes good old fashioned camouflage works best."

"How long have you lived here?"

"Me? All my life. The village was founded right after the floods receded, leaving this canal. My grandfather was one of the founding fathers. They dredged it for fishing trawlers and built the gate."

"Impressive. It's kept you safe all this time?"

"Mostly." His expression darkened. "We've been raided, but we learned to adapt." He also watched the trees. I wondered what monsters he could imagine out there.

A monkey-like creature hung from a branch over the water and gobble-gobbled at us like a turkey as we slipped past it.

"Vulture monkey," Liam said.

"Cute."

"Not much meat on them."

"Right."

We cruised for another ten minutes, listening to the hoots and caterwauls of the forest creatures. Twice, I saw movement in the shadows. My hands gripped the boat's gunwales until I thought I might break off splinters of wood. The canal narrowed, and I sucked in my breath, as if that would help us pass through the thinning gap. Branches scraped against the mast and sail. We passed through a second stone gateway, and then like waking from a dream, the canal widened to a bay with Ors Village sprawling along its banks.

iam guided the boat into a perfect landing at a wharf running along the shore. The boat barely kissed the dock before he leapt off to tie it to the moorings. The sun was setting behind us in a brilliant tapestry of reds. I tossed my bag onto the deck, then climbed up after it.

"Give me a few minutes to settle her in for the night," Liam said, "and then I'll bring you up to meet the elders."

I nodded and turned to inspect the terrain. The forest had been cut away to expose a hillside where a clutch of houses huddled together like a family around a hearth. I marveled at the tenacity of these people. To build in the Inbetween meant constant vigilance, not just against monsters and marauders, but against the encroaching forest.

A couple more fishing boats were tying up farther down the wharf. A gray-haired man handed off baskets of fresh-caught fish to three young children. The rest of the town seemed quiet, like the sleepy lull after a good meal.

Nesi's communication with the elders hadn't been clear. It said only that the village was plagued by vermin, possibly grubs. I had packed a pan-pipe just in case it was rats, but I saw no signs of infestation.

"Ready to go?" Liam asked. He stood close and his magic zinged over me like a warm wave. A shiver went through me.

"You cold?"

I turned to him and smiled. "I'm fine. Take me to your leader." I'd always wanted to say that.

"Ha! You sound like one of those old alien invasion movies."

I was stunned. "You've seen those?" Even in Montreal, most people had never seen movies from before the wars. I didn't expect a homesteader to remember them.

"In the off-season, we scavenge a lot. Came across an old library a few years back. Had a bunch of movies on disk and the equipment to watch them too. The elders set up movie nights once a week for the whole village to enjoy them. I like the alien flicks best. My favorite is the one about the guy who makes a mountain out of his mashed potatoes. You seen it?" I nodded, and his expression darkened. "Of course that was before the troubles began. Now we can't waste our ley-line batteries for such frivolities."

"Troubles? You mean the infestation?"

"That's only part of it. But fishing has been poor for many seasons now. I'll let Uncle Charlie tell you about it. There he is now."

Charlie Geary was the contact name I'd gotten from Nesi. I turned to greet the older man who came down the village's only road with the swagger of someone who spent most of his life on the deck of a boat. His brown hair was salted with gray and curled around his ears like Liam's. Lines weathered the skin above his beard, making him seem older than he probably was.

I held out my hand. "Kyra Greene."

"You the exterminator?" He didn't shake my hand. Instead, he looked me up and down. "I expected someone a bit…"

"A bit more male?" I asked, dropping my hand. I wanted to kill Nesi right about now.

"A bit more. That's all," Charlie said. He rubbed a hand over his stubbled chin. "What we really need is a witch."

I looked around at the placid little village that seemed to melt into the hillside as the sun set. What kind of infestation required a witch?

Liam saw my expression and said, "Let's get our guest fed at least, before you start spouting off your theories, Uncle."

Charlie grunted his approval. As we headed up the road, I noticed details that showed the village wasn't as prosperous as I'd thought. One roof was patched with a piece of blue tarp. Another house had boarded-up windows on the second floor.

The day had been hot and most front doors were open to let in the cool evening air. Women and children watched from open doorways, with accusing eyes. I felt like a prisoner being led to execution. A woman in baggy pants and a dirt-streaked blouse looked up from where she was pulling up carrots in her garden, saw us and startled. Two small children were playing in the dirt beside her, and she ushered them into the house.

"Not a particularly friendly bunch, are they?" I said.

"Don't worry. They're just not used to outsiders. The only strangers most of them ever see are raiders coming over the fence."

I glanced around. I couldn't make out the fence in the fading light, but it didn't seem polite to ask about village fortifications.

Charlie led us to a long, low house that crouched on the uppermost edge of the hill. A woman waited for us in the yard. Her round cheeks were reddened by wind and sun, and she squinted as if it was high noon instead of near dark. Her arms crossed over a thick waist and she wore a sack dress of indeterminate color with a stained apron over that.

Liam kissed her cheek. "Aunt Tess, this is Kyra Greene."

Before she could answer, a boy of about ten or eleven burst from the house.

"Liam! Look what I got!"

Tess saw the meter-long snake wrapped around the boy's hands, squeaked and hustled back inside, her plump arms pumping in stride.

"Sean, you scared Auntie!" Liam scolded. Charlie just chuckled and followed his wife into the house.

Sean grinned. "Sorry. But isn't he cool? Can I keep him?" The boy was Liam's mini-me, down to the long-lashed brown eyes and stubborn curl around one ear.

Liam examined the snake with interest. "I don't know. What do they eat?"

Sean shrugged. "Dunno. We could try some of Auntie's apple cake, I guess."

"That's a garter snake. They eat worms, slugs, and bugs, " I counted off on my fingers. "But not cake. And it's a female. Maybe getting ready to lay her babies." I crouched down to his height and admired the green and black snake. "Do you know garters are one of the few snakes to have live babies? They don't lay eggs."

Sean's eyes went wide. "Wow! You know a lot about snakes! Are you the exterminator lady?"

"Uh, sort of." I would have to clear up that misconception soon. "I'm Kyra. And you should probably let this mama-to-be go."

Liam patted Sean's shoulder. "You can play with it for a little longer, but then you should listen to Kyra and let it go, okay?"

"Okay." Sean dashed off into the garden.

"He's really cute. Your brother?"

"Yeah. He's a good kid, but high-energy."

He waved his hand to show that I should precede him into the house, then followed me into a large room with a fireplace at one end and two comfy-looking chairs before it. A fire danced in the hearth despite the warm evening. A table long enough to seat twelve filled the rest of the space.

Tess appeared, carrying a tray with teapot, cups and a selection of breads and jams. "Charlie is just washing up. You'll be hungry. I expect you all missed supper."

"Thank you." I accepted the tea, a thick slice of brown bread and a pot of apple butter. The simple fare reminded me of the meals in Asgard. That memory brought another brief, stabbing thought of Aaric. I swallowed the tea like I was eating rocks and put down my cup.

I turned to find Liam watching me. He was slim and auburn-haired, nothing like the blond, blue-eyed, brawny Aaric. So why did meeting his gaze feel so poignantly familiar?

"Not hungry?" he asked.

I smiled and felt my lips wobble with the effort. "Just a little woozy from the boat. I guess I am a wardie."

Liam picked up the loaf of bread and ripped off a chunk, then set the loaf back on the tray.

Tess gasped. "Liam! Have you no sense?" She grabbed the loaf and turned it over. "Laying the bread upside down is bad luck! Are you begging the gods for a smack behind the ear?"

Liam laughed. "Oh, Auntie, you know I do it just to get your guss up."

Tess humphed and smoothed her apron over her lap. "One day, you'll push it too far, then you'll see."

Liam picked up the butter knife, grinned at his aunt, and then deliberately stirred his tea with it. Tess shook a fist at him then stomped to the kitchen.

"You're just as bad as Sean," I said. "I take it stirring your tea with anything but a spoon is bad luck too."

"May the gods rain down fire on me." Liam licked tea off the blade. "You'll find the elders here are superstitious. Don't whistle into the wind or you'll bring a storm. Don't let the dogs near the fishing tackle. And never, never say goodbye to the men before they go out on the boats."

"Bad luck?"

"Bad, bad, bad."

"You don't believe it."

His dark eyes darkened. "I believe that if the gods want to take you to Fiddler's Green, then stirring your tea properly won't stop them."

I wanted to ask him about Fiddler's Green, but Charlie arrived, his face even redder than before, as if he'd washed up with a pot scrubber. He sat in the chair closest to the fire with a groan.

"Trading didn't go so well?" Liam asked.

Charlie gave one curt head shake. "Those Huberts are a selfish bunch."

"Hubert is the next closest fishing village, east of here," Liam said for my benefit. "We heard they found a bulla and Uncle Charlie went to secure scavenging rites."

"Or at least trade for a new engine," Charlie said. "Bill and Derek's boat won't last much longer without one." He poured himself a mug of tea and slathered jam on a generous slice of bread. Then he took his time chewing and sipping, studying me until I felt decidedly uncomfortable in my skin.

"I wanted to thank you for this job," I said, more to fill in the empty space under his glare. "Why don't you tell me what kind of vermin I'm dealing with?"

Before Charlie could speak, a wailing sound penetrated the cracks around the windows. It rolled down the chimney and blew in through the open door. It was a cry that rubbed the hairs on my arms the wrong way and tightened the muscles in my neck.

A cry of all-encompassing sorrow.

It built in tempo and octave and decibels until the windows vibrated and I wanted to shed my skin. Then it cut out, leaving the room abnormally silent.

Charlie thrust a finger at the twilight sky outside the window.

"That's why I wanted a witch. I need you to kill that gods-damned banshee."

I cleared my throat. "I just want to make one thing clear, sir. I'm not an exterminator."

Charlie chewed his jam-slathered bread and continued to study me from under his thick brows. Liam leaned in, blocking Charlie from my line of sight.

"Uncle Charlie's just baiting you. The banshee's not the real problem."

"Says you." Charlie snorted.

"Says anyone with a bit of sense. Ignore him, Kyra. You're here for the rockskippers, not the banshee."

"Rockskippers?" I had no idea what those were.

"I'll show you." Liam turned so he spoke only to me. "They come out at night."

"Funny how the banshee only wails at night too," Charlie said. "Some might call that a co-eeen-see-dence."

"Uncle…" Liam said in a warning tone.

I cut in before the argument escalated.

"The same holds for your rockskippers. I won't kill anything. In my experience, extermination rarely works in the long run anyway. Best to find the root cause of the infestation and come up with a solution." That came out more confident than I felt. I didn't know if I could help them with these rockskipper creatures. Liam sat grinning beside me like I was a circus side-show act that amused him.

"Well, Nesi said you could get the job done," Charlie said. "He ain't steered us wrong before. So I don't care how you get rid of them. As long as they're gone, you'll get your money." He dropped a small gold coin on the table. "Half now. Half when the job's done."

I scooped up the coin, trying not to seem eager. It would feed and house me for a month. Two months.

"Great. Can you show me to my room? I'd like to rest. And then I'll need someone to wake me when these rockskippers come out."

Liam glanced at Charlie, who shrugged like it was no business of his. Then he rubbed the back of his neck and wouldn't look at me.

"We thought…well, we thought Nesi would send a man." He finally met my eye. "And the only spare room is at my place."

"Your place?"

He rushed on. "Unless you want to sleep here by the fire. I'm sure Aunt Tess can make up a bed."

"No, that's fine." I would be professional about this. "I just didn't realize that you had your own place. I thought you lived here."

"You'd think so," groused Charlie. "The way he's always here eating our food. You need a wife, boy."

"Yes, Uncle. I'll just go raiding the Huberts and bring myself home a captive bride."

"No need to be a smart-ass."

"Always better than a dumb-ass." Liam sucked back the last of his tea and rose.

Charlie glowered at his nephew, then drained his cup and refilled it from the bottle of brandy Tess had included on the tray with the teapot. "Just go on and get settled. I expect those vermin gone by the end of the week."

I bit my tongue to keep from making any such promise and followed Liam back into the night.

"MY PLACE IS this way." Liam touched my elbow, and it zinged like a tiny bolt of lightning. The full moon was laced in orange as it rose above the tree line. Our feet crunched on the gravel path, a rough sound in contrast to the soft lap-lap of water against the dock.

Tess and Charlie's house was the centerpiece of the bay, as befitted the home of the village elders. Liam led me to a cottage on the farthest edge of the village where the bay thinned out to the canal and flowed back into the great river.

"You live here alone?"

He grinned. Moonlight caught the roguish glint in his eye.

"You'll be perfectly safe," he promised. "But you could go back and sleep on the floor in front of the hearth at Charlie's."

"No, I just mean, why don't you live with your aunt and uncle too?"

"Used to. But last year, Auntie decided I'd have a better chance of finding a wife if I had a house of my own. So I moved back into my parents' old place."

"Oh. I'm sorry. I mean, not that you're looking for a wife, or can't find one. Or whatever. Just that your parents are gone."

We'd reached his front porch and Liam leaned against the rail of the stairs leading up to his front door, a smile tugging at his lips.

"That was the best babble I've heard in a long time."

I felt my cheeks heat. "Can we just go inside now?"

"How about a nightcap first?"

I nodded. Any excuse not to be alone with him in the cottage just yet. There were two Adirondack chairs set on the sagging porch. I sank into one. He opened the front door without unlocking it first. How nice to live in a place without locked doors. In Montreal, I locked the doors even when I was home.

After the long boat ride and the constant vigilance in the Inbetween, home seemed like a distant memory. I hoped that Evelyn, my upstairs tenant, remembered to check on my rescues. It was the first time I'd left them alone. It occurred to me that if I began taking more of these overnight jobs, I'd need to find permanent help. Or get rid of my critters. I wasn't sure if I could do that. My rescues were the only family I had.

The cool night air kissed my overheated cheeks. The river curled silver arms around the village, and I filled my lungs with its fishiness. My keening pinged with the life bustling through the forest that crept right to the edge of the village. I liked the feeling. In the city, the humans and fae were overflowing with emotions—good and bad—that tainted their magic. Here, in the Inbetween, the forest was full of tiny, bright spots of pure magic, brief lives busy with their own importance and not likely to bother us.

Liam returned with two earthenware cups. He handed me one and sank into the other chair. I sniffed my cup.

"It's whiskey. And not home brew. The good stuff. I found it while scavenging a few years back. I've been saving it for a special occasion."

"This is a special occasion?"

"Definitely." He clinked his mug against mine. "It's a marauder's moon." He saluted the blood-red full moon with his mug, but his eyes never left mine.

I took a small sip, and the fiery liquid burned a trail past my heart.

"Are you ever going to tell me about this infestation that I'm supposed to deal with? So far, the only thing I've seen overrunning this village is fresh air and good company."

Liam nodded and tapped my mug again.

"I'll drink to that. There isn't any better place to live in the entire world."

I thought of the beauty of Asgard, the white tips of my grandfather's castle shining against a backdrop of green hills and snow-capped mountains. We always think our home is the most beautiful. And perhaps it is.

"You have to see the rockskippers for yourself. Nothing I can say would do them justice." He leaned his head against the chair back and closed his eyes. We sat listening to the water slough against the rocky shore. I was ridiculously aware of Liam's body beside me, his long thighs man-splayed in the low chair, the curve of his shoulder and strong, bare arm resting on the armrest, close enough to mine that I could feel the heat coming off his skin. In the dark, the shadows aged him. It was a good look, more rugged, less boyish. I pulled myself away from those thoughts again.

Just a customer, Kyra. Keep it business casual.

I gulped my whiskey and sputtered at the burn.

Liam turned his head without lifting it off the chair and looked at me. "Not a whiskey drinker, I take it."

"Not so much."

I felt a sudden need to fill the silence.

"So have you had any luck? Enticing a wife, I mean."

Liam's eyebrows rose, taking years off his life. Enough to remind me painfully of our age difference.

"I'm sorry." I covered my face with my hand. "Awkward small talk is my superpower."

He laughed, a low sound that reverberated through me like a wake-up bell.

"It's okay. I get it. Our life here must seem very isolated to you."

"Not really. I haven't always lived in Montreal. Before that…" I hesitated. "Before that, I lived in my grandfather's house. It was rustic, in a way." In truth, Baldyr's castle was rustic only in its lack of electricity. I couldn't tell him about Asgard. Or rather, I didn't want to tell him about Asgard. It was a private part of my life that I hadn't shared with anyone.

"Rustic I can deal with," Liam said. "But the isolation of living in such a small village can be…difficult. It's hard to think of the girls you played in the mud with as women. You know what I mean?"

I nodded. The village had about thirty houses. That meant a hundred people, maybe a hundred and fifty. It was pretty insular.

"What about the other homesteader villages?" I asked.

"That's the plan. Find a hot older woman from another land." He nudged my elbow with his. "How am I doing so far?"

"And how old do you think I am exactly."

"I don't know. Twenty-five maybe?"

"And that makes you what?"

"Twenty-two." He leaned into me.

The Aesir all looked young, even the ones who were centuries old. But gods, twenty-two. He was just a baby. Thanks to the healing powers of Asgard's famous Golden Apples, I might have looked no older than mid-twenties, but there were fifty years separating us. Fifty years, two distinct ways of life and only inches of breath as he leaned into me.

I pulled away.

"Sorry." Liam sat back heavily in his chair. I couldn't see his eyes in the shadows, didn't want to see the emotion lurking there. Regret, sorrow, peevishness—none of them suited me at the moment.

"Thanks for the nightcap. I'll head to bed now." I rose and waited for Liam to follow. "You'll wake me if these rockskipper things arrive?"

He hesitated a moment as if he had more to say, then nodded.

"Of course."

Once inside, Liam closed the screen, then a heavier wood door.

"It will get warm in here tonight, but I don't dare open the windows.

Those buggers can climb walls. You wouldn't want to wake up with your bed full of rockskippers."

"No, I wouldn't want that." Part of me still believed he was exaggerating the infestation. We stood in his front hall, almost nose to nose. His whiskey-tinted breath warmed my cheek.

"Your room is over here. It's small." He didn't move away when he spoke. I could feel myself leaning in to him, and I stepped back, putting space between us before I made an ogre-sized mistake.

"Thanks. Can I clean up first?"

"Of course. No indoor plumbing though. I guess it's pretty rough compared to what you're used to."

I followed him through a sitting room to the kitchen area. He handed me a washing bowl and a towel.

"I'll get you some water from the well. There's an outhouse out back, if you need to uh…you know…"

"Pee?"

"Right. That." His discomfort was adorable.

"Lantern's here." He took a storm lantern from a nail on the wall and lit it with a brand from the wood stove.

"You should go now, before the rockskippers make an appearance."

I thanked him and took the lantern.

Half an hour later, I lay in a narrow bed in a room that had once belonged to a young boy, by the few toys and books on the one bookcase. For a long time, I watched the marauder's moon rise and disappear above the house.

Eventually, I slept.

And woke abruptly, not knowing why. I sat upright in bed, the blankets strangling my legs, wrapping me in dread. My hair had come loose from its braids and stuck to my sweaty neck. Had I been dreaming? Something that upset me enough to push me into wakefulness? That was possible. The dreams about Aaric smiling as he pushed my blade into his heart had lessened, but not disappeared.

But no. Something else had woken me.

The wind wailed through the trees. Branches scraped at my window, their *scritch scritch scritch* only adding to the unease that rippled just beneath my skin. The wailing escalated.

Not wind. Banshee.

Somewhere on the hill above the village, the banshee cried. Her song skated across my nerves like an untrained bow across a fiddle. I hugged the blanket to myself.

Liam appeared in my doorway.

"They're here," he said. "The rockskippers."

"What time is it?" I covered my bare legs, feeling foolish for my shyness. I'd gone to bed in shorts and a t-shirt, knowing I'd have to get up in the night.

"A little after three." Liam's dark form was a shadow against other shadows.

The banshee's cry rose to a crescendo, sending a wave of goosebumps up my back. When the lament ended, I keened its magic clinging to the night, not willing to let go.

I slipped out of bed and hastily re-braided my hair.

Outside, all was quiet and still except for the repeating slap of waves against the shore. Then the slapping sound grew to a squishy din, like hundreds of feet marching in wet galoshes. I strained to see the water's edge in the darkness. A line of glistening shadows broke along the shore. The black mass oozed across the ground, making for the homes that lined the bay.

"What in the hells?"

"Kyra Greene, meet the rockskippers." Liam grinned, enjoying my astonishment. "Come on."

As we got closer, the mass dissolved into slick black bodies, all struggling to make it to land. They were about the size of a bullfrog, but longer, with tapering bodies and bulbous heads. Two flippers in the front and two in the back flapped at the ground, propelling them forward. I leaned down to inspect the frantic, flailing bodies.

"Are they fish or frogs?"

"A bit of both, maybe. With a good dose of slug thrown in. Too bad there's no good meat on them or we'd never have to take the boats out again."

A rockskipper landed on his shoe with a wet slap, and he shook his leg to dislodge it. A dozen more surged across our feet. Hundreds of them, thousands, all beating their tiny fin-legs to win a place on shore. They were slimy and disgusting and amazing.

"We'd better get back inside." Liam stepped back. "They're a bit overwhelming at night. By morning, they'll be worn out and you can get a better look. Careful you don't step on one. They're slippery."

He took my hand and led me to the house, sweeping the slug-like creatures out of our way with his foot.

When we made it back to the porch he said, "Tea?"

"Yes. Thanks."

He went inside and I turned to watch the incredible infestation. Now I understood the need to keep the windows closed. They were almost at his front door. A lake of pulsing, pushing, panicking bodies.

And I had absolutely no idea how to get rid of them.

By dawn, the rockskippers covered the dock, the road, the porches. They snailed up stairs and cottage clapboards and clung to windows. In the dark I hadn't seen the bright red spot on their heads. Standing in the morning light, it looked like a field of poppies glistened between village and water.

An odd smell hung in the air, like rotten fruit.

I sipped my tea and watched the sunrise slowly frosting the treetops. Two fishermen made their way down to the dock, grumbling and kicking the creatures out of their way. A boy and girl of about eight were plucking them off their front porch and chucking them into the road. It looked like a daily chore for the little ones.

I crept down to the shoreline to study the creatures more closely. Since the children suffered no ill effects from handling them, I crouched to pick one up. It filled my palm like a ball of cold pudding. Two black eyes punctured its red bulbous head, and it watched me with a vacant, fishy stare. Then the creature ballooned to twice its size and let out a noxious puff of breath.

Yuck.

Now I knew where the rotten-fruit smell came from. Flipping it over, I saw a mouth on its belly. After several hours out of the water, the flippers had hardened and atrophied. I put the creature back on the sand and watched it slide toward the water. Looking around, I realized that the entire brood was inching toward the river, despite the atrophied fins. The rockskippers had a second mode of locomotion. Fascinating.

Nesi's right. I should start a critter blog.

Maybe if I had the backing of a ley-line social network, I wouldn't be coming at this problem completely blind. I had no clue how to get rid of these rockskippers, and no way to connect to the ley-line web to research. I had to use whatever tools I'd brought with me.

Like the pan-pipe.

I fetched it from my pack, sneaking past the kitchen where Liam was fixing breakfast. Back outside, I wet the mouthpiece and blew a low note. My piping skills were limited, but a pretty melody wasn't necessary to work the magic. I blew a few more notes, letting them fill the morning. Birds stopped chirping in nearby trees. Several rockskippers turned ponderously away from the river, searching for the source of the magic that called to them. That was all the confirmation I needed. I put the pipe away, not wanting to lure the poor creatures away from the water before the sun desiccated them.

At least I could control them. But could I divert them from the village like the Pied Piper leading rats from Hamelin? It seemed like a stop-gap measure. I needed a better plan.

The screen door slammed behind me and I turned to meet Liam coming out of the cottage.

"These are amazing creatures." I scooped up another rockskipper. "They're amphibious, but see this? Their lower half is just like a slug's foot, and they ooze across the ground on a trail of slime. I suspect they come ashore to eat insects and plant debris in the sand."

"You are a most unusual woman." Liam nodded toward my hand, still holding the gelatinous lump. A grin tweaked his lips.

"Why? Because I find creatures fascinating?"

"Because you're not afraid to dive in and pick one up."

A scream broke the morning's calm. Two doors down, a woman ran from her cottage, her shouts coming in gasping spurts.

"It was in my bed! Oh, gods!" She threw a rockskipper and swiped at her clothes as if they were covered in bugs.

Beside me, Liam laughed. "Finally gone through every man in the village, Janey? Are you now taking beasts into your bed?"

Janey stopped screaming and turned on Liam, her brow drawn in fury. She was young with a well-worn prettiness, blond hair messed from sleep and her thin nightshirt showing curves hardened by muscle. She glared and stamped her foot.

"Liam Geary, you are hateful!" Her eyes flicked to me before she stormed back inside, slamming her front door.

I raised an eyebrow at Liam.

"She'll get over it. But not before she spikes my ale with something nasty." He leaned in as if to whisper a secret. "When we were ten, I slipped a toad down the back of her shirt. She didn't speak to me for a week. Then I found a big fat worm in my soup and all was forgiven." His eyes sparkled. "Come on. Breakfast is ready."

Sitting on the porch, we ate bowls of hearty oatmeal topped with dried fruit and honey, and I considered the lives of these homesteaders, so different from those who grew up within the protection of the ward. No one had secrets here for long. I'd had that kind of tight community in Asgard, and a sudden longing for my home and family hit me. The porridge stuck in my throat, but I forced it down. I wouldn't insult Liam's hospitality by wasting food.

"I'm going to find that banshee this morning," I said.

Liam frowned. "Why?"

"I think Charlie is at least partially right. Last night, when the banshee wailed, it felt like a calling."

I shied away from telling him my pan-pipe confirmed the rockskippers reacted to magic. Letting homesteaders know you carried a magic artifact of that worth was a bad idea. Liam didn't seem like the thieving kind, but I preferred to keep my secrets.

Liam scraped up the last of his oatmeal and pushed away his bowl.

"Some of the elders believe the same. Charlie and Tess included."

"But not you?"

He shrugged. "I think banshees wail and rockskippers skip. It's just what creatures do. No point in making their actions into some kind of magical rite."

"Maybe you're right, but…" I hesitated.

"Go on," he prodded.

I dove in. "I can sense magic, sort of. And there *was* power in that banshee's cry. The rockskippers could be drawn to it."

He studied me and I willed myself not to shrink under that gaze.

"All right. If you're hunting banshees, I'm coming with you."

"You don't have to—"

"Have you ever been into the Inbetween?"

I shook my head.

"Then I'm coming."

CHAPTER

7

Liam packed us a light lunch and added a bundle of fresh wild leeks to his backpack.

I made a face. Raw leeks weren't my favorite picnic fare.

"An offering for the banshee," he said. "*If* she'll see us. This may be a fool's errand."

"An offering? That makes her sound like a god."

"Well, a gift then. A token of our appreciation, or a payment for any advice about the rockskippers."

He also added two knives to his belt and slung a bow and quiver over one shoulder. He eyed my sword in its sheath.

"Know how to use that thing?"

I nodded and tried not to squirm under his scrutiny.

"Good. You'll need it."

I didn't tell him that I would only unsheathe it under the direst of circumstances, and even then, I'd probably let myself be killed rather than wound another living creature with it.

By the time we left the village, the rockskippers had all slunk back to the river, leaving no traces behind except that tangy rotten fruit smell. Most of the fisherfolk had already left in their boats, and now children came out to play.

We hiked up the only road, more of a well-worn path that wound up the hill behind the cottages until it hit a stone wall.

"That's your fence? Does it run all the way around the village?" I turned to scan the forest. The fieldstone "fence" rose three feet above my head and looked

102

solid. It was a feat of engineering I didn't expect from simple homesteaders. But then, maybe these villagers had the chance to live simply because someone in their past had erected this protection for them. I keened a bit of a ward magic in the wall. Not enough to keep out the real nasties, but enough to turn away unwanted human visitors and the encroaching forest.

"It was built in my great-grandfather's time. Took twenty men two years to raise it."

I could only imagine living out here for two years, spending each day at this grueling task while fighting off marauders, vampires and the myriad Inbetween carnivores big enough to take down a man.

"Eight people lost their lives building it." Liam watched me from under his brow, and I felt like he was delivering some kind of test. "But they built us a haven. That's why the elders approved the expense to bring you here. The rockskippers destroy our gardens and get into our water supply. If we can't get rid of them, we'll be forced to leave Ors. No one wants that."

Great. My job just went from simple pest control to saving the fate of an entire village. Clearly, I needed to raise my rates.

"Well, I guess we'd better get this sorted then." I motioned for him to lead on. A few steps along the wall, we came to a heavy wooden gate, reinforced with steel bands. It took us ten minutes to shove open the gate because of the thick foliage on the other side.

"We try to come this way and clear it once a week," Liam explained. "But the forest claims it back almost immediately." Using a machete, he slashed at the vines choking the path on the other side of the wall. For over an hour, we worked slowly uphill, stopping often to cut away branches. For once, Liam didn't fill the space between us with idle chatter.

Finally, the trees cleared and we stood in a small dip in the hillside. A boggy pond filled most of the clearing with a bluff rising up behind it, and a cleft in the rock hinted at a cave.

Liam crouched on the edge of the tree line. "That's where she lives. The banshee."

"Why are we whispering?" We were here to find her, after all. Might as well announce our presence.

"Because of that." Liam pointed.

What I'd thought was just a mud-covered boulder rose out of the pond on four massive legs.

"What is…" The creature cut me off with a roar, displaying an impressive maw with the blunt teeth of an herbivore. That wasn't reassuring. Hippos were herbivores too, but they killed more people than lions. At least that had been true once. Inbetween hippos? All bets were off.

I ducked back into the underbrush and grabbed Liam's arm.

"What is that?"

"Grote-slang." His down-turned grin was just a bit mocking.

We poked our heads out of the bushes again.

The beast stamped forward and shook its head, slinging mud in every direction. It was as big as a cow, but with the diamond-shaped head of a snake. My critical mind took in the details in a few seconds. Round body. A lung capacity big enough to stay under water for long periods of time. Thick legs with claws for gripping the ground. If it had to, this creature could run. And it probably used its mammoth head as a battering ram.

The grote-slang shuffled forward making deep grunting noises and swinging its head.

"Stay behind me." I pulled my knife. It was a good hunting blade, but looked woefully short when held up against the beast. "As long as it's in the water, we have the advantage. If it makes for shore, get ready to run."

Liam wasn't running. He unslung his bow and nocked an arrow.

A second grote-slang popped out of the water and then two more smaller ones. A mated pair. Not good. They were defending a nest. No way they would back down.

"Why don't you draw your sword?" Liam said through gritted teeth.

"Long story," I whispered back. "If we live through this, I'll tell it."

The biggest grote-slang pounced forward, displacing a wave of water. Liam and I crept backward, but I didn't want to run and risk forcing it to chase. The grote-slang opened its mouth wide enough to swallow my head and hissed out gobs of spit and pond scum.

"Enough of that!" A gaunt old woman dressed in black rags came out of the cave to stand between us and the beast. She swatted it on the nose with her bony hand. "Mind your manners."

The grote-slang grunted air out of its flared nostrils hard enough to blow back the woman's hair, and then it sank back into the pond. Mate and pups followed until only their eyes peeked above the waterline.

"You've got to show 'em who's boss, is all." The woman sniffed and turned the full force of her glare on us. "Now what do you want?"

She stood no taller than my shoulder. A dragonfly flitted around her face—a drab gray face, deeply lined and with green in the creases like moss grew there. Hair lank as seaweed hung about her thin shoulders. But it was her eyes that captivated me. They were deep-set, dark violet orbs that drew you in. I couldn't look away and immediately ramped up my psychic wards, suspecting witchcraft.

The banshee stepped forward and poked my shoulder with a sharp finger.

"No need for your protections, girlie. I won't bewitch you."

Interesting. The banshee had the keening too.

"Now stop gaping and tell me why you've come." She sniffled and tears leaked down her face through the mossy crags.

I stood straighter and didn't shy away from her gaze. "We came to ask if you know about the rockskippers."

While I spoke, she looked me up and down, assessing me as a threat.

"Well Liam, you've finally hooked yourself a big fish."

Liam flushed, just enough to reveal the truth of the banshee's insinuation.

She hiked up her ragged dress and turned back to the cave. "You'd better bring your friend in for tea then."

We edged around the pond. I kept a sharp eye on those grote-slangs. Before we hit the cave entrance, I grabbed Liam's arm, holding him back to whisper, "You didn't tell me you know the banshee personally." But he just smiled.

Liam liked to keep his secrets close too.

Inside, the cave was surprisingly cozy. A small fire burned in a hearth below a natural vent. There were no chairs or table, but reed mats were spread on the floor. A bundle of blankets in one corner marked a sleeping area. And above that, on a stone shelf, sat a dozen well-used paperback books. Wow. Real paper books were expensive, if you could even find them. I scanned the titles but resisted the urge to pick one up and thumb through the pages. They looked like they'd been read dozens of times.

"I brought you a gift." Liam dug through his pack. He handed over the bunch of wild leeks. The banshee sniffed them.

"Thank you, child. Those will make a decent stew tonight."

The dragonfly had followed her inside to zip around her head. Up close, I saw it was more pixie than dragonfly. It had jewel-toned wings and a humanoid body with graceful limbs, but a featureless face.

"There's more." Liam handed the banshee something wrapped in canvas.

She brushed aside the pixie-fly and unwrapped the canvas, pulling out a book. It was one of those bodice-rippers with a glistening man-chest and a swooning, gowned lady on the cover. The banshee's eyes went wide. She fingered the precious paper, then gently rubbed a gnarled hand across the cover like she was smoothing the hair away from the face of a loved one. Her mouth opened and she let out a howl that I felt down to my toes. The cry bounced around the cave. She drew it out to a piercing note that leaked away to nothing like a trampled bagpipe.

The banshee sniffed but didn't bother to wipe away the tears etching into the deep lines of her face. Then she might have smiled. Her lips didn't move, but I glimpsed joy in her eyes.

"Thank you for the offerings. You're a good boy." She patted Liam's hand. "Aren't you going to introduce me to your friend?"

"Of course." Liam touched my elbow. "This is Kyra Greene. Kyra, this is Gita…I'm sorry ma'am. I don't know your last name."

Gita sniffed. "Don't have one. Don't need one."

She set her new book beside the others—it was a battered copy of *The Flame and the Flower*, I now saw—and went to the pot hanging over the hearth.

"Had some tea steeping before you woke the grotes. Should be ready now." Gita dipped two chipped, mismatched cups into the pot and handed us each one. It smelled more like broth than tea, but I took a tentative sip and almost choked on the fiery brew.

Liam watched me with a grin before sipping his. The tea tasted like it was brewed from onions, garlic, chives and every other plant in the allium family. Now Liam's gift of leeks made sense.

I took another sip and Gita nodded with a self-satisfied smirk. "It will put hair on your chest and fire in your loins."

"Just what I need." Miraculously, my sinuses cleared for the first time since allergy season began.

"Now sit." She pointed to the grass mats before the fire. "And tell me why you would brave the dangers of the wilds to visit an old woman."

I settled on a mat. The onion tea was growing on me and I drained my cup. Liam's magic had calmed as soon as we entered the banshee's cave. He now sat beside me and slightly behind, giving me his silent consent to take the lead.

Gita crouched by the fire. She scooped a cup of tea for herself and then sat cross-legged like she was about to lead a yoga class.

Before I could speak, she let out another nerve-shredding wail. The magic in that cry wasn't quite a calling like the wail I'd heard last night. I didn't feel any direct purpose in it. It was a pure release of magic, but it made me think of all the myths I knew about banshees. They were harbingers of death. They could whistle the wind and call up terrible storms. Some stories said they could scream loud enough to rupture blood vessels in their enemies, causing a quick, if bloody death.

The wail died away and Gita sat placidly with her hands in her lap. The pixie-fly settled on her knuckles. It was as big as her hand and seemed unaffected by the wailing, while I hugged myself, trying to hold my parts together.

Gita turned her sharp eyes on me as if we hadn't been interrupted. "So what do you want?"

"Kyra has a theory about the rockskippers that have infested the village," Liam began, but I silenced him with a touch on his arm.

"Miss…Gita, why do you cry?"

"Am I crying?" She wiped a hand across her cheek and seemed surprised when it came away wet.

"No, I mean your wailing. Does it have a purpose?" I didn't want to insult the banshee, but I had to know if she understood her own magic.

Gita frowned over my head at the bright crack of light coming through the cave entrance. "It is the song of my people. I am the only one left to sing it." She was looking at a past horizon that we couldn't see.

"Does that mean there were more…of your kind once? Where did you come from?"

Gita came back to herself and glanced slyly at me from under her wrinkled brow. "You ask a lot of questions. Must be my tea loosening your tongue."

"I'm sorry." I handed her back my cup. "Your tea is excellent. I've never tasted anything like it. And I don't mean to be rude. I'm just interested. I like to know about other peoples. Life inside the ward can be pretty dull."

"A wardie, are you? What brings you out of your gilded cage?" She filled my cup again and handed it back.

"The village elders hired me to rid them of the rockskippers."

"And you think I have something to do with those vermin."

I nodded, not wanting to insult her further.

"Well, it may be so." Gita shook her head and a lank lock of hair fell across her face. "You asked about my people. We banshees have always been solitary creatures." She thumped her chest. "But that doesn't mean we have no family. I followed mine from the Old Country to Cape Breton over two hundred years ago. And then here after the great floods.

"They revered me once, like a goddess. Kept my idol on their hearth to remind them, and I felt their prayers in my bones. In return I warned them of death, so they could prepare, but now no one listens."

"So you wail when you sense death is near?"

"Once I did." Her chin dipped and her shoulders bowed. The pixie-fly fluttered upward to land on her shoulder. "But now, without believers, with no family to care for…the urge to sing overcomes me, and…"

I waited out the next wail, sipping tea and trying not to run. The sound felt like nails scraping the back side of my eyeballs.

Gita's cry trailed off and the cave fell quiet again.

"So the crying is involuntary?" I asked.

Gita sniffed. "If you like."

That wasn't good news. If the banshee was responsible for calling the rockskippers from the water and she couldn't stop herself from wailing, then the only solution would be to get rid of the banshee.

"Well, thank you for your time." I rose. "We won't disturb you anymore."

"Tisn't anything like a disturbance." Gita rose too and wrapped long bony fingers around Liam's arm. "You come again soon?" Her voice held a note of hope.

Liam covered her hand in his. "I will."

Gita nodded and wiped her nose on a ragged sleeve.

Outside, the sun seemed even brighter after the dark cave. We blinked our way past the grote-slang pond and were halfway down the path when I stopped him.

"You still haven't told me how you became friends with a banshee."

Liam ran a hand through his messy curls and smiled. He was beautiful. My heart swerved, making a detour around my resolution.

Oh, no. I refused to feel anything for this man. He was too young, too full of hope and expectations for someone as jaded as me. And in two days, I'd be back inside my ward. Safe in the sanitized city where I belonged.

"Hey, wardie, I'll tell you my secrets, if you tell me yours." He took my hand. His fingers were rough and warm against my skin. "But first I want to show you something amazing."

We came to a well-used road, but instead of turning onto it, Liam crossed it and plunged into the bushes on the other side. Then he turned to cut a path that ran parallel to the road.

I was fairly fit, but this hike was more than my wardie legs were used to. I paused and pressed two fingers into the stitch in my side.

"Why don't we use the road?"

"Marauders." A sheen of sweat covered Liam's forehead and his cheeks, already tanned from days on the water, were flushed. He looked older. Or maybe I was just coming to terms with his youth, setting myself up to feel all right about this…*thing* growing between us. He was an adult, after all.

"Don't worry." He continued to break our trail. "It's just a precaution. There aren't many marauders around here anymore. And the opji don't hunt these parts in the fall."

"Opji?"

"Vampires. They breed humans like cattle." He frowned. "But you'll be safe with me. I promise."

He was true to his word. Soon we found a deer path and made better time. As the noon sun tried to shine through the thick canopy, we left the trees and…

We stood on the brink of a village.

A main street started at our feet out of nowhere. The pavement was cracked but clear of debris. Storefronts on either side were well-preserved, the windows dirty, but intact.

"What is this place?"

"A bulla. You said you wanted to see one." He made a sweeping bow. "Your wish, my pleasure."

I was reluctant to step on the asphalt, like that would somehow break the spell and this magical town would disappear. Liam took my hand and gently tugged me onward. Just like our trip through Barrows, he narrated everything we saw.

"I think this town was called Picoudi. At least that appears on several old signs. Look." He pointed to a storefront with a faded sign that read "Marché Picoudi." Picoudi Market. He pointed out a gas station, a deli, and a library with Grecian columns and imposing stone stairs leading to a double oak door.

"That's where I found Gita's book. It's full of them. Movies too."

Standing in the town square, I turned in a circle to take it all in. Except for the missing people, Picoudi looked like it could open for business at any moment. I walked over to the market and peeked inside the window. The shelves were stocked with goods.

I stood back, squinting into the sun. "How does this even exist? It's so… perfect. Like stepping back in time."

"Uncle Charlie explained it best." Liam leaned against a street lamp. "When I was a kid, I got a metal splinter in my thumb from an old fishing reel, and my thumb healed over it. About a month later, it swelled up. Aunt Tess told me to soak it in salt water every day. After a few days, my thumb split and a red ball erupted from it." He made a disgusted face. "It was pretty gross, but also kind of amazing. My body created a cyst around the splinter, to protect itself from the foreign object. Charlie says bullas are just like that. Terra surrounds them in a bubble to protect herself and then spits them out. Come on. I want to show you something else."

I thought about his words as we walked down the jarringly familiar street. I had grown up in a neighborhood just like this. I half expected to turn a corner and find my friends playing basketball in the park.

"You talk like a believer," I said. "Like you think the idea of Terra-the-god is real."

Liam shrugged. "There are worse things to believe in. The really amazing thing is that this place wasn't here a week ago. I come by this way on my scavenging route all the time. No one knows why Terra suddenly tosses out one village while others remain hidden."

"It's a scavenger's dream."

"Yep. I haven't told the others about it yet. I'll have to bring a crew by to take what we can. There's even medicine in the market. We're always in need of that. But I wanted some time alone to explore first." Liam rubbed his windswept curls.

I could understand. This was a magical place. A land out of time.

We spent the rest of the afternoon exploring and scavenging. It was like being on the set of a period-piece movie. I saw brand names I hadn't thought of in years, even my favorite diet cola that I'd practically lived on my first year of middle school when I thought forty-five kilos was too fat.

In the hardware store, Liam packed a duffel bag with tools and ropes.

"These are pure gold. We'll use what we can and trade the rest in Barrows. It will mean my village won't go hungry this winter, even if the summer catch falls short."

"Are you expecting it to?"

"Probably. We catch enough perch and bass to feed the village, but we make our real money on the draika."

"What's that?"

"Big fish." He held his hands wide. "A water dragon. If you're lucky, you'll see one tomorrow when we go fishing."

"I'm going fishing?" I didn't know how I felt about that.

"Of course you are. Can't send you back to civilization without the full homestead experience."

"I'm not here on vacation. I've got a job to do." Bad enough I'd wasted an afternoon at the bulla.

"Pfft." Liam waved away my arguments. "Carpe diem, seize the day, live like you were dying. You can pick your mantra, but you don't want to miss out on my last surprise." He grabbed my hand again and enticed me down the road with his laughing eyes.

About half a kilometer later, the town cut off as abruptly as it began. But the last building was a restaurant with a dark neon sign that read "O'Tooles."

Stepping through those doors felt like stepping back to my teenage years in the early millennium, on those few occasions that Mom offered to splurge on a fancy dinner. To me, "fancy" had meant a pub like this.

A layer of dust covered everything, but the place seemed in order. Booths lined one wall and a dozen tables filled the space before the bar that spouted beer taps for brands that were long extinct.

Liam ducked behind the bar and came back with a bottle of wine and an opener. Then he took a dishcloth from his pack and wiped the table before setting out our lunch.

"You've been planning this since this morning," I accused.

"Maybe." His eyes twinkled with mischief. "Can you blame me for wanting to show a lady a good time? I can't let you go home thinking us fisherfolk are all bumpkins." He laid the cloth aside and opened the bottle. "Sit."

I pulled off my sword harness and laid the sheathed blade across my knees. My right foot bounced, and I pushed down on the sword to still it.

"We might find glasses back there, but…" Liam took a swig of the wine and handed me the bottle.

"That's okay. I don't mind sharing."

He watched my lips cover the head of the bottle. As I drank, his Adam's apple bobbed as he swallowed hard. I'm not ashamed to say I enjoyed his reaction. It had been a long time since I felt that feminine power over a man, that power to make him look at me with honest desire.

I nibbled on fresh berries and looked around at the decor of old street signs and sports memorabilia tacked to the walls. The air inside was hot and stale and seemed to press down on us. I decided to fill it with talk.

"You never told me how you met the banshee."

He leaned back in his chair. "I came looking for her after she wailed away the storm that almost killed my father."

"She can do that? I thought her powers were prophetic."

"Most people think so. But that day, there was a terrible storm. The Inbetween is unpredictable like that. Boats went out on a clear horizon. An hour later, we were in the middle of a hurricane. The elders huddled with all us kids in a storm shelter to wait it out. I heard them talking. They thought none of the boats would come home."

Liam took another gulp of wine and handed me the bottle.

"Your father was lost at sea?"

He shook his head. "No. They all came home that day. Thanks to the banshee. She came right down to the village and wailed into the storm. We could hear her from the shelter. Tess went to see, and I snuck out too. Gita faced the full force of the wind and biting rain and she screamed." He shivered. "The storm turned tail and ran like a scared deer."

I believed it. I'd keened the power in Gita's cries.

"But your dad. I thought you said…" I cut off my thought. Maybe his father wasn't dead. Maybe he'd run off and abandoned his family. I didn't know if Liam would welcome dredging up his family's past.

"Like I said. All the men came home safe that day." He ate a bite of bread and washed it down with wine, but his eyes weren't focused on the meal. "You know, my da never went out on Thursdays because that day belongs to the god of storms. He never whistled and if he cracked an egg on board, he made sure to crush the shells up good so no witches could ride them. He did everything right." He paused. His eyes lost their softness. "Then he went out on a sunny day, not a bad omen in sight, and dropped dead of a heart attack without a bit of warning."

"I'm so sorry." I laid my hand on his wrist where it poked out of his shirt. He looked surprised at the touch, then covered my hand in his.

"It was a long time ago. I was just a lad. But I learned my lesson."

"And what was that?"

"You can take all the precautions, but if the gods will it, they'll take you anyway."

"I'm so sorry. How old were you?"

"Twelve. Sean was just a baby. We went to live with Charlie and Tess after that."

"Until Tess decided you needed a wife."

"Exactly." He grinned and tipped the bottle at me in a salute. "But a few months after that storm, I went up the hill to find the banshee. I wanted to thank her for getting my father home safe, even if he died. She saved a lot of sailors from the Fiddler's Green that day."

"Fiddler's Green? You mentioned that before. What does it mean?"

"Oh, just another of those superstitions. The place a fisherman goes when he dies. A place full of green fields and dancing, good ale and friends."

"Valhalla."

"Just like that. The hall of heroes, but for fisherfolk. A man must be baptized by a life at sea before he's welcomed to Fiddler's Green. I like to think that's where my da is now. He sure put the hours in on the water." His smile was tainted with sadness. Liam wasn't as immune to superstition as he thought. "Anyway, I've been visiting Gita ever since. I bring her little things from our scavenging. She likes books." He passed back the bottle, and I was shocked to see it was nearly empty. My chest felt full and toasty, and Liam seemed to sway a bit. Or maybe that was me.

His fingers found mine and wrapped them in his warm grip.

"So I've answered your question. Now you have to answer one."

His thumb circled mine, reaching into the sensitive palm. Who knew that such a slight touch could be so sexy?

"What do you want to know?"

He leaned down, his lips only inches from mine, and whispered, "Why do you carry that big-ass sword if you never use it?" He reached for my other hand, where it gripped the sword in my lap.

I jerked back in my chair. An icy hand of dread chased away any flirty feelings.

The sword in question—the one I couldn't leave at home if I tried, the one that was always strapped across my back even though I would never dare to use it against a living being—that sword clattered to the floor.

I kicked the chair away.

The sword hummed. It loved to be the center of attention.

"Hey! Slow down. What just happened?" Liam's brow wrinkled. He held his hands up like I was a wild beast that needed calming.

"I'm sorry. It's just…"

Liam handed me the bottle, and I shook my head, taking a swig of water from my canteen instead. I reached down and picked up the blade, willing it to calm down. Then I took a deep breath and ordered my thoughts.

"My sword is special. It's hard to explain to a…to someone who can't sense magic." I almost said "to a mundane," but I despised those derogatory terms that put people into senseless categories.

"It's a Valkyrie blade." I waited to see if that term registered with him, but he continued to watch me with that steady gaze. "It doesn't matter. Let's just say, we're bonded in a way. And I don't like people to touch it." Especially since the last man to touch it committed hari-kari on it.

"But you're afraid to use it because…"

"Because it also has magical properties—properties that certain people find attractive." Certain immortals, anyway. And I'd vowed never to let myself be the instrument of another person's death-wish again.

Liam screwed up his nose in confusion. "I'm not sure I get it."

Words stuck in my throat. He was too nice, too normal. How could I tell him about my soul-sucking sword?

"Let's just call it a family heirloom."

"So you carry around a sword you can't use because it's family heirloom that's bonded to you."

"Something like that."

"And no one's allowed to touch it."

"Exactly."

My fingers drummed on the sheath. Liam sat back. He was shrewd enough not to press me, but cunning enough to keep me off my guard with a new topic from left field.

"So, wardie, do you think you'd ever like to try the homestead life?"

I looked up into his soft eyes. The right side of his mouth smiled, and the left eventually caught up.

"Maybe I would."

He saluted me with the bottle.

"I'll drink to that."

We left Picoudi in the heat of the afternoon. We'd traveled farther east to visit the bulla, and we returned to the village by a different route. The forest felt more like a jungle with humidity weighing us down and flying insects taking off with chunks of our flesh in their teeth. I ducked under a branch and paused to listen to a hissing rumble coming from ahead.

"What's that?"

"A treat." Liam paused, his machete in his hand, bare arms shining with sweat from the effort to cut through thick foliage. "I can see the heat and bugs are getting to you."

I swatted away yet another mosquito disguised as a pterodactyl.

"You mean you like losing half your body weight to sweat and the other half to blood-suckers?"

Liam laughed. "Come on, wardie. We're almost there."

A few more cuts through the forest-jungle and I realized the rushing sound was water. We finally broke through to a small clearing with a pool at the base of a waterfall. Cool spray washed over me, and I dropped my backpack full of scavenged goods. Sword, pants, and boots followed, and I dashed into the water clad only in my underwear and shirt. I dove and swam three strong strokes, coming up at the base of the waterfall. A cluster of eyeballs on fuzzy green stalks clung to the rocks. They all turned to watch me as I floated by.

Not creepy at all.

Then two people came through the spray from the waterfall, and I back-pedaled furiously before recognizing them.

"Liam! Look what I caught!" Sean held up a fat orange fish in two hands. He wore swim trunks and his skinny boy's body was tanned. Charlie, also in shorts, held out a net to catch the fish. His sopping beard and hair looked like a family of wet rats had nested on his head.

"The boy's a natural tickler," he said.

"Look!" Sean dropped his fish into the net, bringing it to shore where Liam waited beside a large plastic bin on wheels. I swam over to see. Liam opened the lid and Sean dumped in his newest catch. The sun dazzled off the brightly-hued fish. Two dozen of them, each about a foot long, and each a different jewel tone. Together, they covered all the colors of the rainbow.

"You caught all those?" Liam asked. "You *are* a tickling wizard. But I'm a tickling fiend!" He grabbed the boy, tickled his ribs and flipped him upside down until Sean shrieked with laughter. Liam kicked off his boots and ran fully clothed into the water with Sean on his shoulder.

"Well, now you've gone and scared away all the fish!" Charlie scolded, but I could see he was amused, not angry.

I dunked myself again to wash away the morning's grit. My bug bites stung in the cool water, but as I swam, those soon eased. Eventually, I pulled myself up onto a rock beside the waterfall, my toes dangling in the water like fish bait, and watched the boys splash and wrestle like feral pups.

Charlie joined me.

"Would you like to try your hand at tickling a fish, if those hooligans ever calm down?" he asked.

"Sure. I've never caught my own supper before."

"Oh, we won't be eating those rainbow beauties. They're for the draikas."

"The water dragons?"

"Uh-huh. Today we catch bait. Tomorrow we hunt dragons." He arched one grizzled eyebrow at me and pointed to the packs on shore that bulged with tools and goods we'd scavenged in Picoudi. "What's that?"

"Liam and I found a bulla. He said it's a new one. There are tools and medicine."

Charlie clapped a hand to his thigh. "It's a good day all round! Liam is a smart young man. He'll make a fine provider. A woman could do worse." He side-eyed me, but I didn't take the big sparkly lure. "Anyway, I hope you'll join us tomorrow on the boats. We'll be leaving before dawn."

"I should stay and try to sort out the rockskippers. That's what you hired me for, after all. And I wasted a day scavenging."

"Scavenging is never a waste. But I think you'll find the fishing enlightening. You can see the rockskippers in their natural habitat. Might give you some insight."

Charlie watched his frolicking nephews as he spoke.

"Okay, I will then. Thank you."

He clapped me on the shoulder. "Good. You can sail out with Liam. He can always use extra hands on deck and you two seem to make a good team."

I forced a smile at his blatant matchmaking. "I look forward to it."

Kyra, it's time...

The voice slipped past me and around me like a derelict wind. I stood in the garden behind my grandfather's castle. In the dark, I couldn't find the face to match the voice. But I knew it.

Aaric called to me.

Kyra, it's time.

I wanted to go to him, but want was precariously balanced on a blade of panic. If he found me, I might find solace in his embrace. And I was so cold. Alone. But if he found me, if he got hold of my sword, if he turned those blue eyes on me...

He'd ask for the one thing I couldn't give.

Wind ruffled the trees. I hugged my arms to my chest.

...it's time.

"Kyra, wake up!"

I opened my eyes to the face looming over me and a scream died in my throat.

Liam. Not Aaric.

"Hey! Are you okay?" His warm hand cupped my shoulder. I struggled to sit up and untangle myself from the sheet. Alarm settled back to the low-ebb anxiety that I'd lived with since leaving Asgard.

Since Aaric forced my hand to be the one that took his life.

I made myself articulate that thought. Put it into words. Put blame where it belonged.

"I'm okay." I smiled. I wasn't okay, but I would be.

Liam stood back as if he just realized he'd invaded my bed.

"There's tea on the stove, if you want something hot, but we should go soon or the others will sail without us."

"I'll be ready in a minute."

"I'm heading to the boat now. Can you bring the cooler on the kitchen table?"

"Sure." My voice sounded far away to my ears.

He watched me for one long moment, his eyes inscrutable in the shadows. Then he nodded and left.

I sank back into my bed, wishing that I didn't want him to join me.

THE ROCKSKIPPERS HAD come again during the night, but they were already slinking back into the water before the sun rose, leaving the dock a slippery hazard. I skidded across it toward Liam's boat and tried to remember if I'd heard the banshee's wail the night before. After the day of hiking, I'd slept undisturbed until the nightmares took me. I rolled my shoulders and stretched my neck from side to side as I walked, trying to work out the tension that had followed me from my dreams.

The men were making boats ready for send-off by loading nets, filling gas tanks, and shouting good-humored banter from one deck to the next.

An old man stood by the dock watching the morning bustle. The corners of his eyes were etched with crow's feet, the mark of a long-time fisherman, but he didn't seem in a hurry to set out like the others.

"Going out on the water with the boy?"

"I am." I smiled but didn't stop, not wanting to encourage conversation. He fell into step beside me, kicking the rockskippers out of the way, while I tried to creep past them, only nudging with my toe when they blocked my path.

"Bad luck to have a woman aboard," the old man said. "I told Liam that. But the young ones need to learn it all over again for themselves."

"I'm sure we'll be fine."

"Uh-huh." He watched me as I slipped on a slime-trail but offered no help. When we reached Liam's boat, the old man grabbed a rock skipper that clung to the bow and tossed it into the river.

"Aren't you the one who's supposed to be saving us from this plague?"

I already didn't like this guy.

"I'm here to investigate the infestation, yes." I bit back a few choice insults and set down the cooler.

"You'll never get rid of them, you know. It's punishment for the sin of murder."

"Murder?"

He leaned in as if to whisper a secret. "Terra does not favor those who only take and never give back. This plague is Her will."

"I'll take that under advisement," I said, not looking around, hoping he'd get the hint and leave.

"Uh-huh."

Montreal Ward was full of Terran fanatics. I'd learned not to argue with them. I opened the cooler and pretended to be busy organizing its contents, ignoring the old man. A tiny pity moth fluttered in my gut. The old guy was probably just lonely, no longer able to join the others on the water. I turned to speak to him, but he was already pestering someone else.

I hoisted the cooler into the boat. Liam was busy at the stern, coiling a rope around his flexed arm. I couldn't help but notice the fluid way he moved. He wasn't bulky, like someone who worked out in a gym. Liam's strength came from hard work in the open air. He was all lean lines with the grace of someone who knew his own strength.

"Don't worry about Brock." He nodded toward the old man. "He's old-school."

I glanced at Brock, who was now berating the brothers on the next boat over. Liam had introduced Bill and Derek to me the night before. They didn't seem any happier to listen to Brock's ranting than I had been.

"He thinks you're all murderers," I said.

Liam stowed the rope in the locker and stretched. "I suppose the fish would consider us murderers too. But people gotta eat." He squinted at me. "You're not one of those vegetable eaters, are you?"

I had been vegan in Asgard, where food was plentiful and the Golden Apples kept me strong and fit. But back in Montreal, I discovered that I was human enough to need a good dose of protein everyday, and protein was scarce.

"No. I eat meat."

"Good. Today, you're going to catch your dinner."

That idea was strangely appealing.

"If you're sure. Brock says my girly bits are bad luck."

Liam grinned. "I like your girly bits." He offered his hand, and I jumped aboard, then saluted.

"Put me to work, Captain."

"You just stay out of my way for now. I'm used to doing things on my own. But once we're on the open river, you can help me set the nets."

One by one, the boats unmoored and slid through the narrow gate in the canal. The trawling motors hummed like a swarm of bees, but we moved only marginally faster than the current.

With the trees blocking the pre-dawn light, the channel was dark and close. I squeezed my eyes shut and trusted Liam to navigate. Then a rush of morning wind told me we were past the canal. I opened my eyes to find the river had opened wide enough to be a lake. The current still drove us toward the ocean some thousand kilometers away, but now it was a deep, fathomless current.

Motors revved and the Ors Village fleet scattered. Sean waved from the deck of Charlie's trawler as they headed north toward the shipping channel, with Bill and Derek's boat close behind. The others plowed east toward the end of the lake, and we idled along the southern shore.

Liam shut the motor and brought in the tiller. "Come. I'll show you how to drop the nets."

The boat drifted on the early morning calm while he showed me how to unravel the net. We worked in silence, bumping elbows and inhibitions in the tiny boat. Then he dropped the oars into the water and cranked them just enough for the boat to surge forward. The nets caught the current and unraveled faster.

Liam saw me trying to slow the output. "It's all right. Let it go."

He rowed for another minute, using the oars to guide the boat. Soon a ring of buoys floated behind us and the entire net was set.

"How long do we leave it out?" I asked. The fishing line had scored my fingers in a couple of places and I wiped them on my jeans. That's why I always wore dark clothes. Better to hide the blood.

"Long enough for us to have some breakfast," Liam said. "And treat those cuts. Come here." He berthed the oars and took my hands, turning them over to inspect the wounds. "See what you need is some good old calluses. Then the nets wouldn't cut you up." His thumb caressed my palm. I sucked in a breath, and not from pain. He pulled a first aid kit from the locker, cleaned the cuts with antiseptic, and bandaged them.

"Thanks."

He didn't let go of my hand, but watched me through half-lidded eyes. The boat bobbed on a rogue wave and I lurched into him. He gripped my shoulders, steadying me. We were three parts of the same beast—him, me, the boat—stirring on the same current. His lips parted like he was about to speak, then thought better of it, and he clamped them shut.

"Is there more tea?" *Award-winning ice-breaker, Kyra.*

"In the thermos." He let my hand drop. "Would you pour us some while I check the nets?"

"Sure."

There was an awkward moment while we tried to pass each other on the cramped deck. Then I doled out two mugs of tea and sat on the locker to watch Liam, bent over the nets. He wore gray cotton pants and a t-shirt that hugged his shoulders. Veins stood out on his arms as he tugged on the net to straighten the line. When he was satisfied, he sat on the stern beside the motor. I handed him his mug, and we watched the sky turn from purple to pink. The other boats were far away on the open lake.

"This is my favorite part of the day." He saluted with his mug. "Just me and the sunrise and the water."

I could see the appeal. The morning sky reflected in the water, shading the light in soft yellows. A flock of cormorants wheeled into view and landed with a spray.

"That's a good sign." He pointed to the birds. "Means a school is nearby."

The weight of the net dragged on the boat and we barely drifted. I took off my jacket to enjoy the sun on bare arms.

"Did you hear the banshee wail last night?" I asked. The tea warmed my belly and it made me think of Gita's onion brew.

"Once. I think. It could have been the wind. You still think she has something to do with the rockskippers?"

"Maybe. It could be that her wail calls to them, like the pied piper and the rats. But I don't believe she's the reason the population exploded."

"Well, maybe you'll have some insight after this trip."

"So where are we going after we bring in the nets?"

He slung an arm around my shoulder. "Anywhere the lady would like to go. Jamaica? Hawaii? The Arctic Circle?"

"Too cold!" I shivered, pretending it was the thought of the arctic and not his touch that caused the reaction.

"Jamaica it is, then. Full steam ahead!"

I gave him a playful punch on the arm. How wonderful would that be to sail off to unknown horizons? It would be a different kind of homesteading, and just as dangerous. But the adventure!

Liam seemed infected by the same whimsy. He gestured to the sky with his mug.

"Wouldn't you like to see what's just over that horizon. In those old movies, people travel all the time. By boat, by train, by plane. It must have been amazing."

"It was. I mean…it does look amazing." I stumbled over my words, not wanting to break the mood by having to explain how I knew about world travel. Granted, I'd left the human realm of Midgard for my ancestral home in Asgard when I was only eighteen, so my experience was limited. But it was still a world and a lifetime away from a homesteader's experience.

An hour later, we hauled the net back on board. It was back-breaking work. Liam gave me a pair of leather gloves so I wouldn't cut myself again, but he tackled the net bare-handed. Every few feet, we'd stop to untangle fish that flapped in the mesh. Liam tossed a few back. These were mostly odd creatures, some I'd never seen before. He rejected a crab-like thing of iridescent green, a flat ribbon fish and two that looked like catfish with a hard shell. Others went into a large cooler near the bow of the boat.

"Is this a good catch?" I straightened, stretching out a cramp in my back.

Liam kept working, as if the weight of the net were nothing. "It's fair. I've seen better. But it'll fetch a good price in Barrows. Bill and Derek will take the haul to town this evening or tomorrow."

"There were no rockskippers in the net."

"No, they'll be closer to shore. Once we've secured this lot, I'll take you to see them."

"And what about the water dragons? What did you call them?"

"Draikas." He squinted into the sun. "They'll only be in the deep. And no net could hold them anyway. Charlie and the others will be fishing for them. There!" He pointed to the middle of the lake.

I shielded my eyes as I scanned the horizon. Two boats huddled together in the middle of the shipping lane where the riverbed plunged to a hundred meters. One of those boats was Charlie's.

"They're hunting draikas right now?"

"Do you want to join them? We haven't seen a draika in months, but the rainbow fish are their bait of choice, so you never know."

I was curious to see the water dragons, but I had a job to do.

"Rockskippers first."

Liam cut the engine, and we coasted around a shoal to a small inlet. The current slowed here as it snagged in the cove. Long-legged herons waded between clumps of grasses. On the shore, a spotted cat the size of a pony drank from the river with both eyes fixed on us.

We drifted in silence and I turned my face to the sun, enjoying the heat as the morning chill faded.

"Thanks for your help with the nets." Liam came to stand beside me. "I usually have to do all that on my own. It's a treat to have an extra pair of hands."

"You're welcome." I looked down at my hands, red from the rough work. I felt good. Strong and clear-headed. Manual labor filled me with a sense of rightness that I didn't get anywhere else. Maybe the homesteader life wasn't so bad.

"So what are we looking for?" I asked.

"Watch." Liam pointed toward a heron. The bird cocked its head, then lashed out lightning fast to snag something in the water. It came up with a fat black and red blob in its beak.

"Is that a rockskipper?" I asked.

"Yup. Used to be I saw one or two rockskippers a season. Now they're all over the shoals around here and even in the deeper water."

"Are they here all year?"

Liam frowned. "I'm not sure. They're worse in the spring and early summer for sure."

"You said they're not good to eat. So you don't fish them at all?"

"Ugh no. I tried one on a dare when I was a kid. It's like eating rancid snot."

"Nice visual." I pretend-gagged, and Liam grinned.

"The herons don't seem to mind."

By now a dozen more birds had come to wade in the reeds.

I studied the little ecosystem, looking for the tell, the one thing out of place that might explain the great numbers of rockskippers.

"Does anything else eat the rockskippers?"

Liam took off his hat and scratched the fringe of hair on his forehead. "Just the draika. But only when they're newly hatched."

Suddenly the water churned, rocking the boat. Reeds swayed as something rippled through them. And then the cove turned into a boiling mass of rockskippers. Hundreds of the fat black bodies were flying through the air, flapping their fins, and clambering over each other in a race for the shore.

"What's going on?" I grabbed the mast as the boat lurched. Liam, whose sea legs were much better than mine, rode out the storm.

"We gotta get out of here!" He pointed into the rising sun, then dashed back to the tiller.

At first, I saw only the morning light glinting off the water. Then I spotted a disturbance, like a train rushing at us under the waves.

Liam started the engine, and we pulled away from shore, but the cove was too small. No way to get out without confronting the advancing beast.

"Hold on!" Liam called. The motor screamed as he opened the throttle. But the little trawling motor wasn't meant for speed, and the boat lumbered toward open water. The beast hurtled straight at us in a game of chicken. At the last moment, it reared up, displaying an impressive bony ridge on its head and a mane of bright yellow tentacles all waving about like the hair of a gorgon. It dove, making barely a splash, and its body undulated past the boat, at least eight meters long. As it turned into the cove, it flipped, revealing a bright yellow underbelly.

Liam let out a hoot and punched the air like we'd just won a contest.

"What was that?" I clung to the side of the boat.

"Draika. Water dragon!"

Water dragon, indeed. "Can you slow down now?"

Liam geared down and grinned at me.

"I haven't seen one in months. It's a good sign."

"Are you going to tell Charlie?" It seemed a shame to kill such a magnificent creature.

Liam must have seen the concern on my face. "Don't worry. That was a spawning female. They go into the shoals to lay their eggs. It's the only time you see them so close to shore. We won't touch her. But when her babies grow up though, they'll be fair game!"

I couldn't argue with that. These people lived by the hunt. We all did what was necessary to survive in the post-war world.

Liam turned the boat northeast, and we found Charlie in the middle of the lake. He'd cut his engine to drift with the current. Bill and Derek did the same about a hundred meters out. Thick fishing poles were attached to both vessels—baited, no doubt, with the rainbow fish. Sean looked bored as he hung over the side of the boat, dangling another line in the water.

"Any luck?" Liam called over to Charlie.

"None. We're down to our last few bait." Charlie was slumped between two fishing poles. Sean pulled up his rod and sat beside him, looking dejected. Poor kid. All that work to catch the rainbow fish and nothing to show for it.

"We just saw a spawning female." Liam pointed back to the cove.

"Really?" Sean jumped up. "Can we go see it?"

"Hold steady, boy." Charlie adjusted his hat and peered at the distant shore. "We don't hunt the mamas, you know that."

"I just wanna see," the boy whined.

One of the rods snapped and disappeared underwater.

Charlie stood, took off his hat, and wiped his face, grinning.

"Well, this might be your lucky day." He pointed to a shadow passing under the boat. Sean whooped in delight and ducked to the other side to watch the draika skim by.

"Liam!" Charlie shouted. "Get out of the way!" Liam put our boat in reverse, clearing a space around the lines from the fishing poles. Charlie spoke into a walkie-talkie and the other boat turned to join us. Bill stood on the rail, a harpoon at the ready. As they closed in, Derek cut their engine and grabbed a second harpoon.

We waited. The boats bobbed. A seagull cawed. The draika sped past again, its long body thrusting up a wave that tipped our boat. I clung to gunwales, my fingers chafing under the rough wood. The dragon's yellow belly flashed in the sun as it lunged at the bait. The pole jerked but held. Charlie grabbed it and hung on.

"There's no way he can reel in a fish that size," I said.

"He won't. That's what they're for." Liam pointed to Bill and Derek, who let loose their harpoons. The draika thrashed as the arrow heads struck. Its tail breached and slammed back down, sending a plume of water into the air.

"They got him!" I couldn't help but get caught up in the thrill of the hunt. Deep down, we're all hunters on some level.

"Not yet." Liam looked grim.

The draika broke the surface like a rainbow-hued battering ram and drove head first into the second boat. The wood splintered on impact, tossing the brothers like rag dolls. Bill hit the railing hard and fell into the water. Derek clung to the rail, another harpoon at the ready.

"Tie him off!" Charlie shouted. He'd abandoned the fishing poles and now wielded his own harpoon, a contraption that looked like a crossbow with a two-meter-long, steel-tipped bolt.

The monster-fish lashed its tail, sending all boats rocking. Sean toppled over the railing.

"Liam!" His scream cut off as he hit water.

"Sean!" Liam was already on the rail, ready to dive in after his brother.

"No!" I yanked him back. "You can't! I don't know how to drive this boat!"

"Damn the boat! That's my brother!"

"I'll go. You keep the boat between us and that beast!"

Liam froze, then realized that his brother had a better chance with both of us working to save him.

"Go." He handed me a life preserver and tied it off to a clamp beside the oar lock. I shucked off my sword but kept my knife handy and dove.

The water hit me like a block of ice. Cold. So cold!

I came up gasping and thrashing. As soon as I got my bearings, I saw that Liam had done his job and put his boat between us and the others. The harpoons had caught the draika, and it churned the water into a bloody stew. I turned my back on the battle and looked for Sean. He was treading water about ten meters away. Waves kept crashing over him and his eyes bulged. By the time I reached him, he was gulping air with only his chin and nose above water.

I pushed the lifesaver ring toward him, but in his panic, he grabbed onto me instead, pulling me under with him.

I'm not a big woman. At five-foot six-inches, most men underestimate me in a fight, and I use that to my advantage. In the open water, I had no advantages, not with a panicking kid who weighed almost as much as me.

"Sean!" I struggled to keep my head above water. Desperate fingers gripped my waist. The lifesaver floated just out of my reach, and I strained to grab the rope. A wave smacked me in the face, and I saw black until I came up sputtering again. This time, I grabbed the rope with one hand. Now I could haul Sean up. He burst to the surface.

"You're okay!" I grabbed him. "I got you." The boy clung to me and the ring. His gasps mingled with sobs. "It's okay. Liam's coming. It's okay."

A shout came from behind me. I turned to see Bill's boat listing to one side, sinking fast. Then a flash of yellow caught the light. The draika breached. Its head soared into the air, making the boats look like toys by comparison. A dozen harpoon shafts stuck out of it like quills. The great body splashed down, sending a shear wall of water over our heads.

Dear All-father, protect me in my time of need.

I didn't think Odin's power reached into the water, but he was the only god I knew personally.

The giant fish wasn't going out without a fight. More blood spilled as it whipped its tail. Then a massive, tentacle-maned head popped up right beside us.

Sean's scream turned hysterical, but he was latched onto the lifesaver, so I shoved him away and turned to face the beast. It opened its maw, full of tiny, razor-sharp teeth. Tentacles menaced about its head.

You can't eat me. I was ten times the size of its normal prey. But it was pissed, and I was the only thing in its sight.

I slashed out with my knife even as the beast attacked. It hit like a like a sack of sand, driving me under and spinning me around so I no longer knew which end was up. I thought I'd made contact, but in the frothing confusion, I lost my knife.

I sank for an eon.

Down down down.

Until the darkness was a solid wall on all sides. I thrashed, looking for the paler wall that marked freedom, air, life. There. A flash of brilliance. Then it disappeared. Not the sun. Just the dragon's yellow belly as it turned for another attack.

My lungs burned, the need to breathe rattling my frozen limbs.

I turned again and again until I found the shining beacon of sunlight.

And I climbed.

I pumped my feet and dragged my arms through the resistant water. My boots were lead weights, trying to pull me into the murky depths. When I finally clawed to the surface, I thought my heart would explode with that first breath.

Sean hugged the lifesaver nearby. Debris from the lost boat floated on the choppy waves.

"Sean!" Liam idled up to us and pulled out Sean first, then helped me into the boat.

"Did we l…lose him?" Sean's teeth chattered from shock or cold.

"Don't worry about that now. Let's just get you warmed up." Liam pulled a blanket from the locker and wrapped the boy in it.

"I don't have another blanket." He rubbed my arms, and then circled me in his warmth.

"I'm fine." I didn't feel the cold. I didn't feel anything. Yet. But I let myself enjoy the moment of contact with Liam.

Then I heard Charlie yell. It seemed far away, like my ears were still full of water. It was something between a scream of agony and a victory shout. The rope of one harpoon was still attached to the deck of his boat. Bill and Derek had abandoned their sinking boat for his, and it took all three of them to haul the beast on board. As soon as its lifeless body hit the deck, it changed color. Gone were the beautiful rainbow hues and brilliant yellow underbelly. It flopped onto the deck and its eel-like body was a dead gray.

12

erek and Bill salvaged everything they could from their boat before it sank to the bottom of the fishing channel. They rode home with Charlie. The carcass was rigged to the boat and streamed behind them like a fluttering scarf in the water.

The draika was even bigger than I had guessed. When they hauled it up on land, the final measurement ranked it at ten meters long, more eel than dragon. Without the waving mane of tentacles, it became obvious that the bony ridge on its forehead also protected a large protrusion on the base of its skull. This was a source of great admiration for the fishermen.

I went inside to change, pulling on dry pants and shirt and adding a sweater over that. My limbs still felt like rubber when I returned to the dock, but my shivering stopped.

Liam finished tying up his boat for the night and came to help the others lug the giant fish ashore for processing.

"I take it draika meat is good to eat." I wrinkled my nose at the pungent fishy smell.

"Definitely. But the oil is the real prize. Looks like this catch is a good one too. See that bulge at the back of its head? Could be forty to fifty liters of oil in there. Pure liquid gold."

"Why's it so special?"

"It burns forever." When he saw my incredulous expression, he added, "Well, not forever, but longer than a ley-line battery. One liter of draika oil can power a boat for a season. It can light a house for a year. And unlike other fish oils, it has almost no smell."

"I see." No wonder they'd fished the draikas into near-extinction.

By the time the last boats were in, preparations were well underway for a village-wide celebration.

The women started a bonfire on the beach to roast fresh strips of meat. The men were already tending blubber pots that would render the draika flesh. It was hot work, but the feeling of community lessened the burden. Someone brought out a keg of beer. Trestle tables were set up and other families brought down breads, jams and platters of fruit and vegetables. Liam handed me a cup of beer and then downed his in one long chug. I took a tentative taste. It was warm and frothy and surprisingly good. I took a deeper sip, and he laughed when I came up with foam on my lip.

"Let me get that." He ran his thumb across my lip, just as my tongue crept out to lick the foam and I tasted his skin instead.

"Sorry," I mumbled.

"S'okay." His eyes sparked with fire in the day's last light.

Around the bonfire, the tale of catching the draika was told, embellished and retold a dozen times. I found myself caught in the middle of these tellings because when they'd pulled the fish out of the water, my blade was embedded deep in its eye.

"Hey ho! For Kyra, the dragon slayer!" Charlie shouted and clinked his mug against another.

"And I'm going to catch tons more rainbow fish!" Sean shouted. "Then we can have roasted draika every night!"

"And a hey ho! For Sean, the best bait tickler there ever was!" Charlie shouted and the others cheered. Sean bounced around the camp, full of energy despite his traumatic day. I wished for such youthful resilience. The river's cold had seeped into my bones and I couldn't shake it. I wore a sweater over my shirt despite the warmth coming off the fire.

"He seems to be over his ordeal already." I nodded at Sean.

"He'll be fine," Liam said. We stood side by side in the bonfire's glow. "You were really brave out there. I don't know what I would have done if I lost Sean."

"It was nothing. I'm used to dealing with beasts of all sizes." I didn't want to make a bigger deal of it than I already had. But I had never faced anything so terrifying.

After we all had a taste of the crispy draika meat, Charlie brought out a fiddle and began a sea shanty that the entire village seemed to know.

"Ho! Hey! Brother, meet at Fiddler's Green!" Charlie sawed the fiddle and chanted.

Several men chanted back, raising their mugs high. "Ho! Hey! Not today. The sun's still shining and the nets 're full."

Everyone joined in for the last line "I'll only come when ol' Lir roars and not a fathom yard too soon."

And Charlie continued. "Ho! Hey! Brother, meet at Fiddler's Green!"

"Ho! Hey! Not today. There's a blue-eyed lass with a kiss for me. I'll only come when ol' Lir roars and not a fathom yard too soon!"

The round continued, with the verses getting sillier until Charlie cut it off with a fiddle solo and couples paired off to dance.

Liam held out his arm. I took his elbow, and he whirled me into a kind of square dance. I didn't know the steps, and we both laughed when I tripped over him. But soon I forgot my awkwardness. His eyes never left mine as he spun us to the tune of the fiddle.

Everything else faded away—the dancers, the fishy smell of cooking draika, the fear I'd swallowed with a mouthful of river water. There was only Liam's soft brown eyes and the warmth of his hand on the curve of my back. My heart hadn't felt so full in years. Not since I left my home in…no. I pushed those thoughts away.

Tonight wasn't for looking backward. I'd done enough of that. Tonight, I had a handsome man, a full belly and a nearly full moon to dance under.

Charlie took a break from the fiddle to fill his beer mug. Liam and I wandered down the rocky beach—away from his house. Eventually, we'd end up there and I would have to make a choice to join him in his bed or not. I wasn't ready to choose. Walking was safe, comfortable, with just that little zig-zag of anticipation to make it exciting.

He stopped and turned to face me. In the distance, I could still see the bonfire lighting up the faces of the villagers. They seemed happy, at peace with the world.

Liam laced his fingers in mine and pulled me close. His kiss was hesitant. I stiffened, but didn't pull away. He grew bolder, parting my lips, inquiring gently with his tongue. He tasted like sunshine, hot and familiar.

After a moment we broke apart, but only by a breath. His eyes searched mine, looking for reciprocation, validation, or just plain old desire.

"You've been on your first big hunt. Tasted draika meat. You're a native Orsan now." His voice frayed at the edges.

"I guess so."

"So when do you think you'll be going home?"

I waited a beat too long to answer, and then I ignored the obvious plea in his eyes and took his question another way.

"You mean when will I finally clear your village of that infestation?" I laughed a bit too harshly and pulled away from his embrace. "Where are they, anyway?"

"They'll come. Look there." He pointed to the river. Two bulbous eyes poked out of the water, watching us.

I bent over to get a better look at the rockskipper, and to put some space between Liam and me. "They're cute, actually. Like a pudding with eyes."

"I don't know. They're kind of—"

He was cut off by shouting from the bonfire area. Charlie gripped Brock by the shoulders. Bill restrained his brother Derek.

"Oh, no," Liam said. "That's Brock Farley. Making a fuss, no doubt."

We ran back to the bonfire just in time to see Brock jerk out of Charlie's grip and point a finger at Derek.

"Terra has punished you, sunk your boat and still you won't believe!" He spat on the ground between them.

"Shut your mouth, old man." Derek's nose dripped blood. He broke free from Bill's grip and wiped his nose on a sleeve. His eyes were black.

Standing beside him, Brock seemed almost childlike. He was thin and bony, shrunken with age, and he barely reached Derek's shoulder, but the angry zeal in his eyes made up for his small stature.

"You're fools! All of you!" He kicked sand on the fire, making the flames spark. "You dance and drink like this is a party! This is no party! Terra sees you all!" He pointed two fingers at his eyes, then around the group of revelers. "She sees what you have done this day. And you wonder why she punishes us with a plague of skippers? You kill her children for what? To light your houses? To run your boats so you can hunt more of her children? A plague of vermin is the least of her punishments. You'll see!"

Charlie grabbed Brock by the arm. "That's enough now. You've had your say, man. Leave it be!"

"Leave it be?" Brock wrenched himself from Charlie's grip. "How can I leave it be, when you murderers will see the wrath of Terra brought down on us all?"

Charlie pushed Brock up the hill toward the cottages until his shouts faded away.

"He's not wrong," I said for Liam's ears only, but Bill heard me.

"What was that?"

I looked at Liam for support. His expression was confused, maybe even hurt. He didn't want me to speak up, didn't want the others to find me disagreeable. Didn't want to break the spell we'd been weaving around each other all day. But I had come here to do a job, and I would do it, no matter the cost.

I stepped into the light so everyone could see me.

"I said he's not exactly wrong about the plague of vermin." I spoke louder this time, and the faces in the crowd were lit ghoulishly by the dying fire. Grumbles of protest broke the silence.

Liam held up a hand. "Let her speak. That's what we brought her here for, isn't it? We all agreed."

I looked around. All merriment was gone. The eyes that watched me were hard, scared, worried. They had come to me for help. My reputation was on the line, but so was their livelihood. I didn't want to sound like a zealot, but they had to know the truth.

"I'm no expert on rockskippers." This brought a fresh round of grumbling. That was the wrong start. I tried again, this time with more confidence. "I do know vermin. Infestations happen for one reason. The creature in question has a population explosion. Rockskippers are no different. Out on the water today, I saw a female draika come into the shoals to spawn. Let me ask you this. What do those baby draikas feed on? They feed on rockskippers, don't they?"

Dead silence met that question. They knew where I was going, and they didn't like it. I let the silence speak. When a few people had the grace to look uncomfortable, I continued.

"Look, I understand the draikas are a major source of your income. And I get that life is hard out here without the protection of a ward, but you've fished the dragons to near extinction. It's time to diversify, to find other sources of profit. Or to live without."

"So you believe that crazy old tree-hugger?" Bill sneered. "Terra brought down a rain of toads because we happen to be good fisherfolk?"

"You brought down your own rain of toads." I shrugged. "But Terra works in mysterious ways."

A long, low wail blew in from the hills behind the village. The hair on my arms bristled as the cry rose, filling the night with caustic music. And just when I couldn't stand the nerve-shredding sound, it cut off, leaving us all agitated in its wake.

"There!" Bill jabbed a finger at the hills. "That is the source of your vermin."

And sure enough, I heard the sloppy *flap-flap* of rockskippers emerging from the water.

The banshee wailed again.

Bill got right in my face and shouted over the noise. "You're a waste of good coin. Can't even get rid of one old banshee, so you blame us."

"That's enough!" Liam got between us and shoved Bill aside. "Party's over folks. Go home."

Inside Liam's cottage, the walls felt too close. I hugged my arms around myself like I was still in the grip of that cold, cold water.

Liam leaned against the kitchen sink. "You really think overfishing of the Draika is the reason for the infestation?"

I couldn't read his expression in the dim light.

"I do."

"What about the banshee?"

"She's a complication, nothing more."

"What do you mean?"

I held up a finger. "Wait here."

I ran to my room and came back with my pan-pipe. I was willing to give up one of my secrets. He'd earned it. "This emits a low frequency magic. Vermin react to it. I tested it on the rockskippers, and they followed the sound."

"Like the Pied Piper."

"Exactly. I think the banshee's wail is the same. It calls to the rockskippers, but it's not the reason there are so many of them."

"Well, damn." He ran a hand through his hair. "I guess that means we'll need to scavenge for gas again. Tomorrow, I'll check out that bulla we found." He glanced at me. "Want to come?"

I shook my head and wouldn't meet his eye. The memory of our kiss hung in the air between us.

"I should go home. I can't help with the rockskippers. Best to cut my losses."

Bill and Derek would bring today's catch to market in the morning. If they would have me, I'd catch a ride with them. It would be back to oatmeal for dinners again.

"Good night, Liam."

"Good night." He brushed a hand down my bare arm as I passed. I wouldn't look at him, but I couldn't deny the shiver of desire that his touch woke in me.

A few minutes later, I lay in the dark, staring at the shadows on the wall above my bed. The wind had picked up, and it tossed the branches outside my window. The banshee's wail mingled with the coming storm—a harmony of death and destruction.

I didn't want to be alone.

It hit me like an arrow to the heart. I was done with solitude. Done pining for my first love, a man who'd strung me along for years and then used me in the most heinous of ways, leaving me with nothing but the burden of his death.

I was done.

I slipped off my shirt and panties and padded into the next room where Liam lay on his bed, arms braced behind his head. In the gloom, I couldn't tell if he slept or stared at ceiling. Moonlight from the open window played across his stomach, highlighting rippled muscles.

I stood in the shadows, naked and goose-fleshed, heart thudding and mind still unmade.

I knew what I could do.

I could slip into his bed, my back sliding against his chest. He'd curl himself around me, his lips finding the hollow between my shoulder and neck, kissing, tasting, nipping down my bare back. I would turn in his arms, fully ready to put away solitude. Ready, willing, wanting.

"Are you coming to bed?" His tone was dark. Not what-are-you-doing-here dark. Sultry dark, like chocolate-covered strawberries.

"Yes."

We made love as the banshee screamed.

13

The rockskippers were gone before dawn. I stood on the empty beach in bare feet, sipping tea. Liam came up behind me, pulled back my loose hair and kissed my neck. I leaned into it, and the kisses moved up my throat. He was solid and warm at my back, and when he wrapped his arms around me...

I didn't want to go back to Montreal.

It was official. I was a homesteader.

A chill wind blew off the water and I shivered.

"Cold?" He hugged me tighter.

"A little." I watched fat clouds race across the sky. "Is it normal for the rockskippers to leave so early?"

"Mmm?" He wasn't paying attention. And if he continued doing that thing with his tongue, I wouldn't be paying attention much longer either. I pushed away and put a hand on his chest. "I'm serious. They're all gone. It that normal?"

He frowned. "No. I guess not."

"The weather's changing."

"Just a summer storm."

"Maybe." I'd been working with animals long enough to know they sensed things we couldn't. Once, all the hounds in my grandfather's kennel started howling for no clear reason. Two minutes later an earthquake shook the foundations hard enough to collapse a wall.

"I think we should get inside." I glanced up again. The yellow light of dawn was fading, but those clouds sped across the sky like a derby horse spying the finish line.

Liam grinned. "The water looks pretty choppy. I guess we could miss one morning's catch for a few more hours in bed." He twined his fingers in mine.

"No one should go out on the river today."

He ducked his head to meet my gaze. "You're serious."

"I am. Call it a premonition. They won't listen to me, but maybe if you tell them…"

"You expect them to listen to me?" He laughed. "If Charlie wants to go out, I can't stop him."

He pulled me up the slight slope toward his cottage. We didn't make it to the porch before the wailing began. The banshee's cry was strident, insistent, more like a fire alarm than her usual mournful howl. People came out of their houses to listen. Janey, who'd found a rockskipper in her bed on that first day, wrapped a robe around herself and ran over to us. She glanced at our interlaced hands and frowned.

"What is that old witch on about this morning?" She nodded toward the hills.

"I don't know." Liam scrunched up his brow. The banshee's cry didn't sit well with him either.

Another woman poked her head outside and frowned at the sky.

"That's a death-watch cry," she said. "She hasn't wailed like that since the storm of '60."

Liam snapped into emergency mode. He dropped my hand and turned to Janey.

"Go ring the bell. Wake everyone. We need to bring the boats in."

Janey nodded and ran off. Others were already heading for the docks. Liam jumped aboard his boat. I stood on shore while he started the engine.

"Tell me what we need to do." My fists clenched with useless energy. I watched everyone rush around with well-prepared efficiency. This was a community that had survived disaster before by working together. I was an outsider, standing like a rock in the middle of the hurry-scurry stream.

"Meet me over there." Liam called over the sound of the engine and pointed to the strip of sand where we'd shared our first kiss. "We're going to beach the boats, if we can. Better than leaving them in the water to get battered by the storm."

He pulled away from the dock, gunned the engine, then cut it. By the time the little boat hit sand, he was already packing away the portable motor. He jumped out, and I helped him drag the boat farther inland.

The banshee continued her lament.

Others were hauling their boats in too. I couldn't see how we'd get the larger ones, like Charlie's trawler, ashore. In the end, we didn't have time to consider the problem.

The weather in the Inbetween is a wild beast. It can be sleepy and peaceful. Then a bee stings its butt, and it rampages across the land without restraint.

"We need to get inside now!" Liam shouted over the rumble of thunder. Icy rain lashed down, stinging my face and bare arms. We ran for his cottage. The wind nearly took the screen door off its hinges before we pulled it shut, then he slammed the heavy inner door.

I wiped rain from my eyes. Liam moved to the front window, leaving a trail of water.

Outside, trees bent to the ground, thunder drowned the banshee's cry. Waves churned up the shore. The wind had pushed Liam's boat onto its side, and the mast dug into sand. The boats that hadn't made it to land slammed the dock. A shutter banged against the house, then a tree branch broke off the great oak outside my bedroom. It crashed through the front window and I jumped back as glass sliced across my bare arms.

Liam ran to the kitchen and returned with a towel.

"It's not safe here." He ripped a strip off the towel and tied it around my forearm. I watched the cloth turn red, not really grasping that it was my blood. "There's a shelter at Charlie's. We'll have to run for it."

I nodded. My heart thrashed around my chest like a fox in a snare. Liam took my hand, and we plunged back into the storm.

The climb up the hill to Charlie's seemed like it would never end. We fought against hurricane winds and slippery ground, sliding one step back for every two forward. When we reached Charlie's sturdy brick house, Liam led me around the back to a cellar door.

"Hurry!" Charlie stood in the rain. Two more villagers were descending cement stairs to the cellar. Charlie braced himself against the wall of the house, squinting into the storm.

"Anybody else?" he called.

"I didn't see anyone," Liam shouted back.

We dashed down the stairs and Charlie slammed the double doors, sealing off the cellar. The sudden quiet was disorienting. My ears still roared, and water dripped into my eyes. I wiped them on my bandaged arm.

A dozen people huddled in the basement that was lined with shelves of canned goods and supplies.

"We'll be safe here." Liam shook water from his curls.

"What about the others?"

"There are several storm shelters in the village. Everyone knows where they are and to take shelter." He smiled and brushed a wet lock of hair from my cheek. "Don't worry, wardie, this isn't our first rodeo."

Thunder crashed overhead, and I cringed. He pulled me in for a hug, and I clung to him, shivering and scared and embarrassed by my fear. When the shivers calmed, he tucked me under one arm, and we went to sit with the others.

The room was lit with a gleam—a precious alchemical contraption fueled by ley-line magic. I hadn't seen a gleam since arriving in Ors Village and guessed they kept them only for emergencies. Charlie and Tess handed out blankets and towels. I sat with my back against a shelf and dried my hair and face. Another elderly couple huddled in the corner beside a young family with three small children. Brock was also there, and two fisherman I recognized by sight but whose names I couldn't remember.

"Where's Sean?" I asked.

Liam looked around the dim room and frowned.

"Tess, where's Sean?"

"He went to Jacob's house this morning. Early. I'm sure Lila has him safe in their shelter."

Liam stood and paced three steps to the stairs. "I should go look for him."

"You're not going out in that storm," Charlie growled. "Sit and calm yourself. The boy is fine. Lila takes care of him like her own."

But Liam wouldn't sit. He paced around the small room, wearing a hole in the floor and on my nerves.

As adrenaline faded, my arm throbbed. I tugged on Liam's fingers as his pacing took him by me again, and he threw himself down beside me.

"Are you worried?" I asked.

"No. Yes." He ran a hand over his wet hair.

"I'm sure he's safe."

Liam smiled at my weak attempt to soothe him.

Tess passed around cups of water. "I'd make tea, but I don't dare light the kerosene down here."

"It's fine. Thanks." I accepted the water gratefully.

She frowned at the bloody strip of cloth wrapped around my arm. "Let's get you bandaged properly."

I let her fuss with my arm. The bleeding had stopped, but the gash was long and shallow. It probably needed stitches. Tess *tsked*, and cleaned the wound with a precious bit of rubbing alcohol, then re-wrapped it.

I thanked her and settled back into my blanket cocoon, glancing at the gleam that was starting to bob in the air as its charge wore off. When it crashed, we'd be stuck in total darkness.

I leaned my head against Liam's shoulder and listened to the storm rage.

Unpredictable was the Inbetween's middle name. The storm blew out as fast as it had blown in. An hour later we emerged from the shelter, blinking in the bright sun. The air smelled earthy clean. Rivulets of water running down the road were already steaming away in the sun, suffusing the village with ghostly mist. Several trees had come down, and debris filled the street—roof tiles, bent and broken outdoor furniture, fishing nets, tools and toys. The villagers didn't bother to complain. They just began the cleanup.

Liam cut across the village, and I followed him. A boy of about ten was picking up branches in the yard of the last house on the lane.

"Jacob, where's Sean?" Liam asked.

The boy didn't look up from his task. "Dunno."

Liam grabbed his arm and forced him to turn. "What do you mean?"

Jacob yanked his arm back. "I mean I haven't seen him."

"He wasn't in the shelter with you?"

Jacob shook his head, his eyes wide as understanding dawned.

"Did you see him at all today?"

"No."

Jacob's mother, Lila, came out of the house, wiping her hands on a towel. "What's the matter?"

"Sean is missing. I thought he was with you."

Lila paled, making her dark-rimmed eyes stand out. "You go check the Gradys. I'll ask at the Fletchers."

We split off to check the other shelters. No Sean. By now everyone had stopped the cleanup effort to look for him. Men and women searched the forest, calling his name. Liam and I walked along the beach and checked all the boats. Those on land had fared the storm well. Charlie's trawler had some damage, but the boat tied next to his rested on its side on the bottom of the canal. Still, we boarded it and searched the small cabin. No Sean.

We stood on the beach and Liam scanned the water.

"Is there anywhere else he could be? Somewhere he would go to ride out the storm?" I asked. Kids always had secret hiding spots.

Liam rubbed his eyes. "None that I can think of."

"What about the falls? Last night he was boasting about catching more rainbow fish."

Liam shook his head. "Sean knows better than to go outside the fence by himself."

Really? No fence would have stopped my ten-year-old self.

"We should check anyway." I kept my tone gentle.

His glance cut across me. If Sean was alone in the Inbetween during that storm…I laid a hand on his arm, trying to will comfort into him with just a touch.

And then he was running up the hill toward the gate.

The forest around the village sustained heavy damage. Part of the stone wall had fallen. Leaves littered the ground as if it were October instead of June. Downed branches blocked the trail that led from the village to the waterfall, and we wasted precious time cutting them away.

Liam didn't speak. He slashed at branches and vines, fury fueling him now. His eyes seemed to have sunken under his bunched up brows. The roar of rushing water grew louder until we broke through the last bramble of debris into the clearing at the edge of the pool.

A body floated at the base of the falls.

No no no!

A strangled cry erupted from Liam. He dropped his blade and dove into the water. Seconds later, he dragged Sean out and dumped him on the grass. He wasn't breathing. Liam pumped his chest, turned him on his side and thumped his back.

None of it would help.

On the rocks beside the pool, knees huddled against his chest, sat Sean's ghost.

Tears streamed down Liam's face. He turned the boy again and pumped his chest. I reached a hand to stop him, but held back. How could I tell him to stop? What were the words that could make someone give up on a loved one?

After another minute, Liam jumped up, turned to the forest and let out a primeval yell. Birds in a nearby tree took to the sky in response to this new and unexpected danger.

He fell to his knees, shaking, growling, weeping. Sean's ghost watched in silence while hurricane Liam raged on.

Finally Liam wore himself out and crumpled to the mud. I crouched and put my arms around him.

"I'm sorry." Pathetic words that didn't begin to encompass the depth of hurt trembling through him.

"Why did he always have to be so stubborn?" His voice croaked from his raw throat. "Why couldn't he just do as he was told for once?"

I knew why. Even in death, Sean's ghost-eyes never left his brother. He adored Liam. Worshiped him. He'd come to the falls because he wanted to prove his worth. The village depended on the draikas to survive. And catching them depended on the rainbow fish. Sean had discovered the one way he could be useful to his family. He wanted to make them proud. To make Liam proud. So he snuck away, hoping to surprise everyone with another batch of draika bait.

And now he was dead.

Just like that.

Inside the ward, people told stories about the Inbetween, about its unyielding weather, terrifying beasts and ruthless bandits. I had only partially believed those stories. Now I'd seen the beauty in Terra's plan to retake the land. I'd also seen the callous brutality of it. This was no longer our world. We would have adapt to that new reality. Or leave this world to those who could.

Liam rose and went to sit beside the body.

"He's too young." He stroked Sean's face, now gray in death.

"He is." I wouldn't force any platitudes on him about a god taking the best to live on with him in heaven.

"No, I mean to get into Fiddler's Green. He's only been on the boats a month. Fiddler's Green takes only fisherfolk who've earned their place in the keg halls of heaven. My da is there and my uncle. But they won't be welcoming Sean. He hasn't earned it yet. Never got the chance…"

He covered his eyes again. Ghost-Sean stood up now, fear plain in his eyes. I didn't discount his belief. After all, Viking warriors believed that only death in battle would send them to the halls of Valhalla, where they would spend all of eternity drinking mead and toasting their glory days. Why should fishermen not have a heavenly tavern of their own?

But there was more than one way to get into heaven.

So I did the only thing I could. I unsheathed my sword and dragged the tip across Sean's forearm, leaving a thin red gash. The blade sang out in ecstasy.

"What the hell, Kyra?" Liam jumped back, pushing me away from Sean. I fell on my butt, my blade still gripped in one hand.

Ghost-Sean smiled, then spread his arms wide. Bits of him dusted away. And in a moment he dissipated like morning mist in the sun.

Valkyries don't just carry swords. We carry soul-suckers. In the battles of old, we walked the killing fields, dispatching those worthy warriors to Valhalla with a strike of the blade. My soul-sucker was the reason Aaric could finally bring his immortality to an end. And now it was the only gift I could give Sean, an easy passage to the afterlife he deserved.

But how could I explain that to Liam? Liam, who gathered his brother's body close to his chest and turned predatory eyes on me.

I re-sheathed my sword. "I did what I had to. He's at peace now. Please trust me."

Liam glared at me over Sean's wet curls. I reached for him.

"Get the hell away from us." His lip curled in a snarl.

He gathered Sean against his chest and lurched toward the path to the village.

I jumped in front of him, and he paused.

"Liam, please—"

We stared at each other. I knew every inch of his body, and yet he glared at me from a stranger's eyes.

"Out. Of. My. Way." His words dropped like stones in a pond, leaving ripples of regret on my heart.

I stepped aside.

I let him go.

At the fork in the path, I made a last-minute decision. Instead of heading downhill to the village, I turned south and continued to climb, working my knife to clear the path.

When I came to the marshy clearing, I ignored the grote-slang's mock bluster as it stamped its massive feet.

"I'm not here for you."

The beast snorted and held its ground, protecting mate and babies camouflaged in the mud.

I rounded the pond and came to the banshee's cave.

Gita sat on a blanket by the fire, feeding it sticks. The pixie-fly perched on her shoulder, its wings at rest.

"He's dead then." Gita spoke without looking up. "The boy."

I nodded, then realized she couldn't see me.

"Yes." I sat on the mat beside her.

"I tried to warn them." She sniffed.

"I know."

"You'll be leaving?"

"Yes. I think you should come with me."

She turned to me. Lank hair fell across her face like wet weeds. Tears streaked down her cheeks and dripped over her nose.

"This is my home. I followed my people here. First to the shores of the new world. Then here. Each time we moved, I left a bit of myself behind. Why should I leave again?"

"They blame you for the rockskippers, say that your wailing calls to them."

I rubbed at my pounding temples. "I'm not sure they're wrong. And now, after this morning. They'll blame you for the boy, say you called the wind with your cries."

Gita sat bolt upright, and the pixie-fly flitted around her head. "I did no such thing! I was warning them. Not my fault they're too stupid to listen. They've forgotten the old ways. That's the real problem."

I nodded. "Even so, you should come with me. It isn't safe here anymore."

She eyed me from under her long hair. "And how will we get there? By boat?"

"We'll walk." I wouldn't go back to the village. Liam would tell them what I'd done to Sean. They were grieving, and I was an outsider, an easy target for their misplaced anger. I would lose out on the other half of my fee, but I hadn't been able to help them anyway. Maybe taking Gita away would calm the rockskippers for a while.

The banshee rose and looked around her tidy cave. "Can I take my books?"

"A few of them. I have books for you at my place. At least I have a tablet where you can download any book you want."

Gita sniffed. "Words aren't real if you can't smell them."

"We'll figure it out." I pulled a burlap sack from a pile beside the hearth and handed it to her. "Take only what you need. It'll be a long walk."

E P I L O G U E

Three months later, a small package was waiting for me at Nesi's shop.

"Comes from Ors." Nesi's one good eye watched me carefully. I'd refused to explain why I'd tempted Terra with an overland journey from the fishing village instead of arriving by boat.

I accepted the package, but waited until I was back home to open it. Inside, I found a pouch of silver coins and a letter.

Dear Ms. Greene,

I am trusting that this letter gets to you. I don't know what happened between you and Liam, but I was sorry to see you go. The boy has always spent too much time looking over the horizon, and I had hoped he finally found a partner to suit him.

He won't talk about your split, and I'll respect his need to mourn privately. Mourn you, that is. We all mourn Sean as a family, and there isn't a day that he isn't close to our hearts and our thoughts.

You might be interested to know that Liam and Janey Rourke were married last week. I'd given up on those two ever seeing each other as anything but rivals. But perhaps it's better that he keeps his heart close to home.

Anyway, I wanted to be sure you were paid for your services. An Orsan always keeps his promise. And you were good to your word. The banshee is gone. I don't know how you did it, but thank you.

The rockskippers keep mostly to the water now, but we still find a few on the docks of a morning. I suspect you are right about overfishing the draika.

And I thank you for the insight that this old man should have been wise enough to grasp long ago. We will adapt. It will be hard, but we are hard people. Hard but not hard-hearted.

I'd like to say you'd be welcome in Ors any time, but I think we both know that isn't true.

Charlie Geary

HELLO, BLOGOSPHERE!

June 10, 2070

This is my first post in what I'm calling the Valkyrie Bestiary Blog. I feel like I'm sending my words out into a great void. Is anyone even listening? I guess only time will tell.

In my pest control business, I have run across a lot of unusual animals. Some defy logic and imagination. Did they arrive here with the fae from Underhill or other worlds when magic bombs broke our world? Or have they always been here, hiding in cracks until the magic was strong enough to come out into the light again?

Maybe we'll never know. I don't think it's important. But these creatures are here now, and I often find myself caring for them, with little or no knowledge of their eating habits or natural habitats.

I know it sounds odd for a pest controller to be worried about the fate of what some people consider vermin. But I am worried. I try my best to treat these creatures with dignity and compassion, re-homing when possible rather than exterminating.

The mission of this little ley-line journal is to find like-minded critter caretakers and open a discourse on fae-creature husbandry.

For my first entry, I bring you a rare pixie-fly that followed me home from a trip outside my ward. He (or maybe she?) is like a dragonfly with bejeweled wings, and the faceless body of a pixie. I found it living in a marshy area, but since I've been home, I haven't found anything it's willing to eat. Any suggestions would be appreciated. The little fly isn't looking well.

Comments (2)

Welcome to the wonderful world of animal husbandry. I have a small menagerie of my own and would love to chat with you about critters. For your pixie-fly problem, I suggest a slurry of mosquito larvae. Or take it back to where you found it. Maybe it eats something rare only available in that one spot.

cchedgewitch (June 11, 2070)

> Thank you for the warm welcome. Unfortunately, there is no going back. I will try the mosquito smoothie. Sounds yummy.
>
> *valkyrie367 (June 11, 2070)*

THREE HALF GOATS GRUFF

June 6, 2079

Ah, middle school—the place where dreams and wonderment go to die.

The gray facade of my alma mater stared down with blank window eyes. Had the architect purposefully designed it to look like a prison or was that just happy chance?

Valiant Middle School hadn't changed. I squeezed past a murder of black clad goths loitering by the front entrance, reeking of teenaged self-righteousness. A gang almost exactly like this one had lurked outside these doors for most of my eighth grade, but I bet these kids thought they were really unique.

"Like the hair," I said to one girl who probably had fae blood judging by her elfin features. Her hair was spiked, colored deep purple and tipped in silver sparkles.

She scowled and stepped into my path.

"Scary," I said and pushed past her. She called a slur after me and her friends laughed. Yeah, she was really tough, and I suddenly felt old. When did teenagers become a nuisance to me? And how long before I started yelling at them to stay off my grass? Thanks to the magic of Asgard, I might only look twenty-four years old (maybe thirty on a bad day), but walking back into that middle school, I felt every one of my seventy-eight years.

Inside, the air smelled stale. Gray walls. Gray floors. Gray air. I turned into the main office and waited for the secretary to finish a phone call, berating some kid's parents for his rude mouth. Finally, she put down her widget and looked at me.

"Yes?"

"Kyra Greene. Valkyrie Pest Control. You have a pest problem?" I flashed an official-looking badge. Along with my uniform, the badge put people at ease. That and a mild glamor let them ignore the sword strapped to my back.

"You're late," said Mrs. Fitch—according to the nameplate on her desk.

A group of students ran by the office squealing with wicked glee. She glared at me as if it was my fault that her school was overrun with kids.

I shrugged. *Sorry, I only wrangle nasty critters, not kids.*

"You were supposed to be here four hours ago," she said.

"I was held up with a nest of cerastes. I can come back tomorrow morning, if you prefer." I wouldn't have minded heading home for a hot shower. And when was the last time I'd eaten? I couldn't remember.

Another group of preteens ran by, yelling and scuffling with each other. Quivers of arrows jutted up from their backs, and one kid had his bow drawn as he sighted the portraits of past principals on the walls. Behind them, a smaller boy tossed an axe in the air and caught it as he followed along.

"No running in the halls!" Mrs. Fitch yelled. The kid with the bow pointed his arrow at her, but Mrs. Fitch glared him down.

Kids might not have changed much in sixty years, but their weapons were better. When I went to Valiant, I'd had to sneak in my one small hunting knife, until I learned to glamor my sword.

But a lot had happened since then. The Flood Wars had reshaped the landscape of the entire world. Billions of people died, and those who survived learned to fight for everything. Kids grew up quicker now. Dodge ball and football had been replaced with archery and—for the lucky few who could call upon magic—spell casting. School wasn't a nine-to-three deal anymore either. I glanced at my widget. It was after seven p.m. and kids were still busy with extracurricular activities. I would have welcomed that distraction as a teen living with a sick mother. School had been my haven and leaving it at three p.m. every day had seemed unfair.

When the kids turned down the hall for the gymnasium, Mrs. Fitch brought her attention back to me.

"We've got goats infesting the creek behind the school. They damaged the property and I want them gone."

"Goats?" Not your typical infestation.

"Three of them." She frowned, turning the lines around her mouth into deep rivets. "At least half of them were."

"You mean one and a half of them were goats?"

I remembered Mrs. Fitch. Well, not her exactly. I remembered her type. During my three years at middle school, I spent much of my time in this office for one infraction or another. The secretary back then had been just as cranky and quick with her dial finger to inform parents of the slightest transgression. Mrs. Fitch could have been her twin. An ancient, grim-faced woman with a frown that could melt granite.

She peered over her silver glasses. "I mean, the bottom half was goat. The top half was…well…boy. Curly-haired boy."

Satyrs. Damn. I could forget about dinner and an early night now.

I took out my widget and dialed my office to check in. Ethan's voice chirped through the earpiece.

"Valkyrie Extermination. If we can't kill it, no one can."

I winced. Ethan was my newest assistant. So far he hadn't run screaming from the job, which was a plus, but he had a dark sense of humor. Maybe too dark.

"Ethan, I think you need to find us a better slogan. Something happier."

"Happier? Like: You find 'em, we squish 'em?"

Sigh.

"Keep working on it. And cancel my appointments for tomorrow morning. I've got satyrs at the middle school."

"Ouch," Ethan said. "Where there's satyrs there's bound to be…"

"I know. Never mind that. Just push all appointments back. And Ethan?"

"Yeah?"

"We're pest controllers, not exterminators." Mostly.

"Right on, Commander."

I closed the line. Mrs. Fitch waited impatiently. She probably had detentions to give out.

"Lead the way," I said.

Mrs. Fitch walked briskly out of the office and down a hall toward the back of the school. The fluorescents flickered, casting a horror-show glow on the amateur artwork pinned to the walls. The quiet halls whispered of the angst and grind of a long history of adolescent trials.

Mrs. Fitch's orthotics squeaked with every step. She led me through a glass door to the back courtyard where I had once hung out with pretend friends, pretending to be cool.

An old man stood on a rickety ladder, painting over graffiti on a garage door where someone had spray-painted a herd of goats. A stick-figure shepherd rode one goat like a bucking bronco while a second bent over the back of another goat in a cartoon rut.

Satyrs were nothing if not predictable. They thought with their pricks. If they could, they would eat, breathe and sing with their pricks.

"This is where I last saw them. Three little miscreants drawing that filth." Mrs. Fitch waved at the garage. Without another word, she returned inside. The door clicked as it locked behind her.

"Hey, Davro." I nodded at the old man. Slowly, he descended, his joints creaking with each step. He took my hand in his and wheezed.

"Kyra."

His voice chafed like nettles and he smelled like a musty cottage. By human standards, he was ancient. Of course, Davro wasn't human. His glamor wavered and, for a moment, a gnarled branch held my fingers before the illusion of a liver-spotted hand returned. I always wondered why he appeared as an old man. The fae used glamors to walk unnoticed among mundanes. They could look like anything they chose. Perhaps Davro used his old-man glamor to go through life unnoticed.

"Things 'ave been quiet 'round here, since ye left," he wheezed.

"I can imagine."

Davro had rescued me when my Valkyrie magic manifested. For the first months of eighth grade, I'd been plagued by extrasensory hearing and an inner sight that left me puzzled. One lunch hour, my new sensory talent exploded and the pounding of every heartbeat in the school assaulted me. The sheer amount of life-magic was overwhelming. Davro found me cowering in the janitor's closet, trying to stuff sponges in my ears. Anyone else would have thought I was crazy or called for the nurse. But Davro knew of my Valkyrie heritage—knew before I did. He called it the keening and laid a hand on my head. I slept.

I woke in my bed with my mother at my side. She explained to me about the keening, the sixth sense that let me hear magic. Then she handed me a rather ugly antique sword, and so my Valkyrie training began.

I learned fast to filter my new magic sensing ability. I had to, or I'd go insane from the constant barrage of magic all around me. Now, that sixth sense made me an excellent pest controller. I could keen the little beasties in the walls without any fancy equipment. Catching them was another matter.

"I hear you've got a satyr problem."

Davro snorted.

"Rats're a problem. Satyrs be a disease. A sexually transmitted disease."

"Any idea why they're here?"

He took a pipe out of his overalls pocket but didn't light it. Davro had given up smoking years ago. He just liked to chew on the end.

"They be tippity-tapping across the bridge at all hours." He nodded toward the creek that ran behind the schoolyard and emptied into Lake St. Louis on the south end of the island. Satyrs loved a good bridge to dance across.

"Troll?" Where there were satyrs and a bridge, there was bound to be a troll collecting his due.

"Aye." He sucked on his dry pipe. "Nasty bugger. Been sleeping for years."

To Davro, years could mean decades or centuries.

"But he's awake now?"

"Aye. I've heard him moaning and groaning under the bridge. I told the kiddies to stay away but," he shrugged. "They don't listen. He's frightful cantankerous that troll."

Trolls were always cantankerous. I was more worried about what had woken it. A ley-line could have been breached under the bridge. Ley-lines criss-cross through the land, like veins of pure magic. The alchemists tapped into them to fuel everything from the cars we drove to the ward that protected the city. But ley-lines could be unpredictable. If one swelled to breaching point—or was purposefully ruptured—it could release enough magic to wake a troll.

Davro stretched out a hand. I thought he would touch my cheek, but he reached past me and laid his fingers on my sword. It vibrated at his touch.

He sighed and stood a bit taller. "That's a live one."

I didn't begrudge him stealing juice from my sword. Valkyrie have always lent power to warriors in battle. It was the second most important purpose of the Valkyrie sword. Davro was no Viking, but he was a warrior in spirit and welcome to the boost.

"Well, I guess I'm off to battle a troll," I said.

"Ye shouldn't battle with trolls. That's an honor they don't deserve." Davro frowned.

"What would you suggest I do? Sing it to sleep?"

"Nay. Ye should kick it in the gunnies and slit its throat while it be down."

Davro, the romantic.

"I'll keep that in mind." I gave him the double-cheeked kiss that Valkyrie reserved for their elders. He bowed his head in a faint gesture of respect and went back to painting over satyr smut.

"Watch for the other," he called over his shoulder. "He be lurking in these parts for a few nights. I don't like his sort."

I had no idea what sort this other might be, but I figured I'd soon find out.

I made a quick stop at my truck to gear up: a tranquilizer gun with sleep-tipped darts, a flare gun, knife, med kit and a roll of duct tape. As an afterthought, I tucked a can of bug fogger into my deep pockets.

Critter wrangling rule number four: There isn't much you couldn't kill, confuse or disgust with a good can of fogger.

Time to flush out some satyrs.

Mother Nature had fallen asleep at the switch. April showers brought May showers and one week into June, the ground squished underfoot like mushy peas. The setting sun lit a band of dark clouds from below, painting the sky in a wash of red and black. Thunder rumbled in the distance, but so far the day had remained dry.

On the far side of the paved courtyard, satyr tracks were easy to follow down to the riverbank.

My grade-eight biology class once came here to discover biodiversity in our own backyard. Back then, this had been a creek, just a thin line of water dug deeply into its habitual path that ran down to the lake. That was before the Flood Wars—before climate change caused land masses to fall into the ocean. Even twelve-hundred kilometers inland, Montreal hadn't escaped a complete reshaping. The Saint-Lawrence Seaway swelled, swallowing chunks of land, and tiny creeks like this one blossomed into full-fledged rivers.

I skidded down the slick embankment into water that reached my ankles. My boots weren't waterproof, but they'd been covered with enough bug guts and slime over the years that water barely oozed in around the laces.

Terracotta Bridge loomed ahead of me, one of dozens of covered bridges hastily erected after the Flood Wars. The red-stained bridge was faded and picturesque, with windows dotting along one side. The satyr tracks headed toward it, but disappeared when they hit water. I could win an easy bet that the satyrs bunkered down somewhere near that bridge.

A clump of grasses growing up through some rocks made a good blind. I hunkered down to wait. The satyrs would show. I'd tranq them, truss them up and cart them off to Dorion Park where they would have hundreds of acres to roam and no impressionable teens to pester.

I scanned the terrain in the fading light. Not a breath of wind rustled the branches. Birds had already gone to roost, and night crawlers were slow to emerge in the damp evening. The world seemed to be in a pause.

I crouched on the stony edge of the river. Little pools dotted the bank, showing just how high the waterline had reached in the past few weeks. A red splotch moved over the rocks in the pool beside me. I let my gaze fall on it, but kept my other senses alert to anything happening at the bridge. A gelatinous head poked out of the pool, followed by two long tentacles that grabbed my boot laces.

"Hello." I reached down and gently unclasped the tentacle. Pink suckers latched onto my finger. "You're much too far from the lake. Did you get stuck?"

The little squid-like creature stared at me with huge eyes.

Lake St. Louis was home to all sorts of wacky and monstrous creatures that made the Inbetween seem like a petting zoo, but it was rare to find any of those creatures so far inland. He'd probably been lured into the river by minnows and crawfish, then been trapped when the water retreated.

I'd read about squid that could thrive in brackish water, and Lake St. Louis was definitely saltier since the Flood Wars, but this far upstream? Surely, the little critter couldn't survive long in this fresh water. But then, what did I know? I could be looking at a mutant cephalopod that ate magic shrimp and pooped out gold nuggets. I'd seen crazier beasts in my time. Still, he didn't look well.

I glanced at the sky. There was no time to bring him back to the lakeshore before dark. I wavered in indecision. I hated to leave him here, but…

A clattering sound broke the silence. Something was running across the bridge. A dark curly head poked through one of the windows and darted back inside. Soon a drum-like staccato of hooves echoed down the river. It was the satyr version of "nana-nana-boo-boo" as they taunted the troll.

I plucked the squid-thing out of the pool and plopped him into the river. He would have to find his own way back to the lake. I had satyrs to catch.

I crouched among the reeds and waited. A light drizzle fell and shadows filled the struts under the bridge. Any minute the troll would rear its ugly head and demand payment from the satyrs abusing his bridge.

Nothing but eddies in the river moved. The gurgling water interfered with my hearing, and I shifted my weight, sinking deeper into the creek. I had other senses to reach out with, but I keened only the natural magics of spring flora slowly coming back to life.

Satyr hooves pounded along the wooden bridge again. I waited for the troll to appear. He had to be awake. Rip Van Winkle couldn't sleep through that racket.

He must be playing with them. I stilled myself—not just my movements but my breathing and my soul—and blended into the background. It was a trick I learned while stalking vermin, and what was a troll but a large, odoriferous varmint?

I waited.

Studying the shadows, I saw him standing against the stone supports under the bridge. I could just make out the silhouette of nose, chin, and the bend of a knee, as if he'd leaned back for a smoke and fallen asleep standing.

The sky was so dark with the indecisive storm that the sun had gone down unnoticed. Lightning flashed in the distance and the creature stepped from the shadows.

Hells' bells, that was a good-looking troll.

Rain fell like a wet blanket, blurring my vision. I resisted an urge to wipe my eyes. I wasn't sure he had seen me yet, and I wanted the advantage of surprise.

"This is not a safe place." His voice was oddly inflected and muffled by rain. "You shouldn't be here." He pushed against the current, one step at a time, closer to my hiding spot.

The moment of decision: in the half light, I could slink back through the reeds and pretend I didn't see him or step forward and confront the being who might or might not be a troll.

I could usually identify a supernatural by the sound of his blood. Mundanes pumped blood through their veins with a desperate economy of heartbeats. But not every creature relied on regular blood flow to survive. The blood of the fae, for instance, didn't course through their veins. It danced, flashing on and off like mating fireflies on a summer eve. Even those with regular heartbeats sounded different to my ears. A gargoyle's beat was the ominous tolling of a cathedral bell. A troll's was cacophonous like a toddler clanging pot lids.

But the stranger was too far away for me to keen him.

"I can see you. No use hiding."

I didn't move. He could be bluffing.

He continued to splash carefully through the river. The rain slowed and I took a moment to examine my potential target.

He didn't look much like a troll. He was tall, lean and well…human. Black hair clung to his head and flattered his sharp features. Water dripped down his face and shoulders as if its only purpose was to accentuate his masculine form. From this angle, his eyes were shadowed as he stared into the reeds that hid me. His right hand held a walking stick, but he didn't lean on it for support, even when the creek's current tossed him off balance. Not a walking stick then. A staff. Possibly magic. Definitely a weapon.

Come closer, my sweet. Just a few more feet…

There. The rain faded and I could hear his heart. It was quiet—almost imperceptible—and slower than humanly possible.

So not human, but not troll.

"Come out, come out, where ever you are," he sang in a passable tenor.

I rose, foolishly wishing that the rain hadn't flattened my hair.

I was hunting tadpoles. Photographing the bridge. Panning for gold. All those excuses ran across my thoughts, but none of them came to my lips. We simply stood, ankle deep in rushing water, and stared at each other. In the last of the day's light, I finally saw his eyes. They were the silver-gray of my favorite cat's belly. He licked rain from his lips, and still we didn't speak.

I wondered if I could ever speak again.

"It's not safe here," he said. "There's a storm coming."

I shook my head and found my voice. "It'll blow over. I'm not worried."

"Still, you shouldn't be here."

"Why not?"

"The runoff. It can cause flash flooding."

Behind him, a satyr waggled his bare ass out the bridge window. I stifled a giggle.

"You think that's funny? Floods can kill." He frowned and I had the irrational urge to smooth the little crease that appeared between his brows.

"No, I think it's funny that we're standing here getting soaked to the bone while a satyr moons us."

"What?" The stranger swung around in time to see the curly-haired menace stick out his tongue and disappear back into shadow.

On the opposite bank, a pile of stones churned and bucked. The water-worn rocks rose and gathered into the rough shape of a man.

Crap, a rock troll.

A tranq gun wasn't going to work on that.

"Get behind me," the stranger said.

I leapt forward, pulling my hunting knife from its sheath. The troll roared, the noise only slightly less offensive than its stench.

"Gods." I heard gagging from behind me, but I couldn't worry about the civilian now. The troll lumbered toward us like a zombie inukshuk. From above, satyrs screamed like little girls.

"Ommmm," moaned the troll.

I slashed with my knife. The shock of hitting stone numbed my arm. The troll cuffed me, a gentle tap that tossed me twenty feet to land in the scrub brush beside the river. While I disentangled from the brambles, the stupid civilian launched his own attack.

The sound of his wood staff meeting stone bounced around the small valley etched out by the river. Hopefully, the rain and descending fog would keep the noise from spreading beyond. I'd had enough trouble with local law enforcement lately and didn't want to explain how I let a stranger get beat up by a troll. The guy was giving as good as he got though. For every three lumbering swipes of the rock troll's fist, he got in at least one parry with his old-man staff that now glowed like heated steel.

I cut my way out of the bushes and stumbled back into the water. The troll had him in a bear hug and only the man's sheer strength kept him from snapping like a twig.

"Ommmmm." The troll's eyes rolled back in his head. The gaping hole that was a mouth spread in a grin. He was getting off on the violence. Gods, I loath trolls.

The stranger gurgled out a few words. I thought I heard "kick him in the rocks."

Sure. I could do that.

I lunged across the water, turning an ankle on slippery stones. *Ignore the pain!* I kicked out, aiming for one of the troll's legs, hoping to take him down. The troll didn't notice, and pain lanced up my foot. My stranger friend was turning an unattractive shade of purple. At least the troll's hands were busy at his throat, so I could beat the beast about the head. Slash left, right. Steel on rock. My knife sheared off with a shower of sparks. Each blow stung my arm but I kept on. He flinched. It was something. I redoubled my efforts. A fly could do more damage to an elephant, but my blows were enough to distract him. He let the stranger drop with a splash. I couldn't take time to see if he fell face up.

The troll's fist came at me. I twisted, taking the hit on my shoulder, but the spin smacked my face against the troll. Blood burst from my nose. Pain speared me and the world tilted. As I fell, the stranger's hands propped me up. He was down, but he made sure I wouldn't join him.

But I'd dropped the knife. My only weapon left was the sword strapped to my back—the sword I'd vowed never to wield against another living thing.

The blade sang its triumphant magic as I pulled it from the sheath. After ten years of confinement, it was finally free.

The troll swung his boulder-fist. I ducked. He lunged. I ducked again. As I gaped up at his solid mass—like a mountain teetering above me—I saw one small crux. Under his chin was the focal point for all the troll's shadows, a darkness that throbbed with vulnerability.

The momentum of my next lunge pulled me upward, and once again I faced his stinking pie hole. He was excited. It's hard to tell with a rock troll since they lack the subtlety of facial expression, but his mantra sped up.

"Ommmm!"

My nose hairs curled in the exhalation that followed.

"Omm. Omm." His fist clenched around my throat. As air left me, I wondered at the massiveness of his hands. Then I could only focus on the sweltering spots before my eyes and the thunderous wave in my ears—my own blood as it shrieked in protest. The troll tightened his grip. An equally hungry hand clenched my calf as the stranger fought against the current.

Light faded from the edges of my sight.

A flash of red shot from the water and I heard a shrill scream.

"Weeeeeeee!"

Mighty squid landed with a splat on the troll's face. The troll released me to claw at his own head. The squid continued to scream, and he'd puffed up to three times his normal size. I didn't know what he was doing, but the troll didn't like it. He flailed and grunted, kicking up rocks and mud. Then the squid fell away, leaving the troll covered in a thick mess of black ink. He roared, trying to swipe the foul liquid from his eyes.

My fingers were numb and my vision blurred, but I keened the hum of my blade—steel mixed with thousands of years of Viking blood and Valkyrie magic. It moved as part of me. I didn't need to feel my fingers on the hilt to flip the blade skyward. One jab drove it into the shadow crux under the troll's chin.

Since the dawn of time, the Valkyrie have been cleaners. After the greatest battles, we swept across the killing fields and tidied souls away from mangled corpses. One strike of a Valkyrie sword brought peace to the mortally wounded. Two strikes sent his soul to the rowdy halls of Valhalla to live out eternity in drunken bliss.

The sword was made for blood. It found the tiny hole in the troll's armor, sunk to the hilt in his brains, and shone gold as it drained the troll's life. I strained for air and held on until the troll tumbled like a mountain into the sea, tossing me onto the rocks.

Blackness.

C H A P T E R

3

I awoke to dark, wet pain. Much pain. My head throbbed. My throat was raw and rocks jabbed me in the back. Gently, I surveyed the damage to my face with shaking fingers. My nose was broken. Someone had set and bandaged it.

The bridge sheltered me from the rain but not the damp. I looked up at the struts of the old structure, lost in shadow now. I lay on a wet bank of stones and mud that barely held back the rushing river. The stranger sat leaning against the struts, tending a fire. Beside him, a hole gaped in the ground. The troll's den.

"You should be in a hospital," the stranger said. "But I figured you wouldn't leave without your sword." My eyes adjusted.

"My sword!" The emptiness in my scabbard itched like a lost limb. I scrambled up.

"It's over there." He pointed upriver. A mound of boulders—all that was left of the troll—diverted the flow. My sword jutted from it like Excalibur.

"I couldn't pull it out," he said. "And I know how your kind are touchy about leaving swords behind."

My kind, huh? We'd have to chat about that later.

The rain had diffused into a soggy mist. Every muscle ached as I stumbled over wet rocks toward the remains of the troll. My sword was wedged in tight under the creature's chin, though you'd be hard pressed to know it was a creature. It now looked like a natural tumble of rock.

My sword hadn't left my side since I was a child, but I also hadn't taken it from its sheath in over ten years. What would this fresh violence do to it?

It hummed a loving note when I gripped the hilt, and the blade slid easily from the stone.

"King Arthur has returned," said the stranger with a sly grin.

"Funny." I scanned the river for a little red face, but the squid was gone. I gave him my silent thanks and plunked down beside the fire, eager for even this bit of dry warmth.

We sat in silence for a while, the kind of silence that only soldiers who have fought together can find comfortable.

"My name's Henry Mason." He held out a hand. I shook it even though his eyes mocked me. "Call me Mason."

"Kyra Greene. Thanks for this." I touched the bandages on my face. A faint tingling under my skin told me that the bones were already healing. Another perk of my long stay in Asgard.

"No problem. You took quite a hit. I should change the dressing."

"I'm fine."

"You're not. Let me look."

Before I could protest again, he plucked the bandage from my nose. His fingers were chilly, but gentle. His eyes penetrated the darkness, and I felt naked before him.

"That's one hell of a shiner." His voice was gruff and his unnaturally slow heartbeat quickened. I ducked my head and my hair fell between us. He tucked it behind my ear. I didn't like the fuzzy feelings his touch stirred up.

"So what kind do you think I am?"

He frowned in confusion.

"You said, 'your kind are touchy.' What kind is that?"

He shrugged. "Adrenaline junkie. Always looking for the next fix."

"You think I chased down a rock troll for the high?"

"That's a Viking sword." He nodded at my hunk of metal. "Not pretty, but good for hacking. What are you, some kind of shield-maiden?"

I bit my tongue so I wouldn't spit out the truth.

Mason shook his head. "Vikings are the worst kind of adrenaline junkies. They always cause trouble for my kind."

"And what is your kind exactly."

"Wouldn't you like to know." He grinned.

No problem. I liked a good challenge. I would figure it out. His magic was slow and steady, eternal like waves crashing on a beach.

"You're a dragon," I said.

He laughed. "Have you ever met a dragon?"

"No, but it's on my bucket list." I studied him some more. "Oh, gods. You're not opji, are you?" I hate vampires. The entire race should be swatted out of existence like blood-sucking mosquitoes.

He watched me from the shadows, and I waited for the mesmerizing magic vampires used to lure in their victims. Nothing. His gaze had weight, but the only thing it affected was my good sense. He really did have amazing eyes.

"Not opji," he said finally, pulling away. "Enough of the fun and games. If you're going to stick around, we have work to do before morning."

"Before morning? Are you crazy? I'm exhausted and that pile of stones will sleep for days. I'll come back tomorrow and put him into stasis."

"Sunrise is in exactly three hours and twelve minutes. Shortly after that, kids will be streaming over that bridge as they head back to school. I aim to have that troll bound by then. You may go whenever you wish."

"Fine. But I left my mage kit in my truck."

"Just like a Viking," he said with a sneer. "Come to a magic battle wielding nothing but a sword."

I let the comment go. It was valid. Viking's were not a subtle race.

"Luckily, I have everything we need." He stirred the coals, scooped water into a small pot and placed it on the hot rocks beside the flames. From a picnic basket, he took out several pouches and sniffed the herbs inside.

"Got any hoagies in there?" I asked. "Battles always make me hungry."

He tossed me a wrapped sandwich. I devoured half of it with two bites. Before my stomach overran my manners, I offered him the second half. He shook his head.

"You need it more than me. I can almost see your wounds stitching together. That must take some energy."

I nodded, too tired for witty quips.

"So how are you planning to contain it?" I asked. "We could scatter the boulders. It would take years for the troll to call them back and put himself together again."

"Years is not long enough." Mason put a pinch of herbs in the pot. A wave of stinking steam rose and surrounded us like fog.

"Ugh. That's nasty."

"Nasty to us, but ambrosia to a satyr."

"I don't get it, I thought we were trying to contain the troll."

"And who do you think woke him in the first place?" Mason said angrily. "The little buggers have been causing mischief all over town. And satyrs can smell troll under twenty feet of rock, which is where I stuck this one last time I contained it."

"You contained it?"

"Yes. Just after this bridge was built. He was a young troll then, easily fooled." He scowled. "I would have lured him back to his resting place again if you hadn't interfered."

"Interfered? I saved your ass!"

He raised one eyebrow at me.

"Is that so?"

"Ya-huh. You were face-down in the water, clinging to my ankles, if I recall."

"I was trying to pull you off him before you did more damage. Now look at him! How do you propose that we move all that rock from there to here." He pointed to the pile of stones that reared up from the river like a cairn and then to the troll den that was slowly filling with water.

It was a monumental task. I shrugged.

"I'm up for it. How about you, werewolf?"

"Nice try. Not a werewolf."

"Were-bear?" That would account for the slow, deep magic. Just like a slumbering bear.

He rubbed the back of his neck with one hand. "Not a bear."

He dropped one last ingredient into the pot, a shriveled root or truffle. The fog turned yellow and thickened. I gagged on the stench. The mist swirled but didn't dissipate. It pulsed with currents like a heartbeat.

"Now what?" Fog muffled my voice.

"Now we wait. You just sit there and look pretty." Mason leaned back against the struts.

I grinned. He thought I was pretty. Of course, he was only being facetious. I looked like the third act of a horror show. My face was swollen and bloody, clothes wet and caked with mud. And my hair—I didn't even want to know.

But he watched me. The fog hid and revealed him in mysterious waves. It swirled around both of us, reaching with delicate tentacles. I closed my eyes. Just as sleep almost overcame me, his voice joined the fog, filling my awareness.

He sang in old French. It was haunting and sweet, like a lullaby for a dying child. The song pulled at me strangely. It compelled me. I moved closer. The fog was so thick now that I couldn't see Mason, but I could hear his heart, steady and slow, only inches away. His fingers reached out and clasped mine.

When the song ended, he began it again. I imagined the sound drifting over the trees, gathering wind and tumbling across fields, up hills, into cracks of old windows and down chimneys.

He was casting a spell.

"They're coming." His grip tightened on mine.

I heard them before I saw them. The questioning tippity-tap of hooves overhead. Fog rolled and shifted. A lanky body dropped from the rafters. And another. The last and smallest crept down the rocks. Three satyrs stood before us, swaying to the sound of Mason's voice. Their hands were idle at their sides, which was the first indication that something was off. Normally, if a satyr had nothing in his hands, they were firmly planted down his pants. I'd never seen one stand still. They were a nervous, giddy breed, but this trio stood like pack mules at rest: heads lowered, eyes half-closed and one hoof at a relaxed bend.

Mason let his song drift off, but its echo went on.

"Easy now." He rose and pulled me up beside him. "Hey, fellas. You want this?" He poured the foul brew into three tiny cups. The satyrs swayed toward him. "You want it, don't you?" They nodded dumbly. The small one stuck one thumb in his mouth and the other hand down his pants.

"You can have it," Mason said. They stepped forward. "Not yet!" They cringed from the whip of his tone. "First I have a job for you." The satyrs pouted. "Come now. It's an easy job for three strong boys. All I need is for you to bring that pile of rocks over here and fill this hole."

"That's it?" The tallest satyr asked. "That's all we have to do and you'll… you'll give it to us?"

"That's all."

"Promise!"

"I promise." Mason crossed his heart.

The satyrs considered.

"Will you sing to us some more?" asked the little one.

Mason smiled. "Of course."

The satyrs moved fast. I didn't register that they were gone until they dumped the first load of stones in the hole.

Mason sang, this time a bawdy tune about barmaids and spilled ale. The satyrs whistled along, laughing now. They tossed basketball-sized stones into the hole with little effort.

"Strong little buggers, aren't they?" My toes tapped and my nose throbbed to the tune.

Mason nodded and started another song, this one in another language I didn't recognize. The satyrs didn't care. They danced and laughed, filling the hole with troll parts.

When done, the half-goats sat at Mason's feet like kindergartners waiting for story time.

"Here it is." He doled out three tiny cups of steaming liquid. "Don't drink it all at once." But his warning fell on deaf ears. The satyrs were already gone.

"What did you give them?"

"It's a bio-hallucinogen."

"A what?"

"Harmless enough for them, though it would kill a human. It stimulates the sexual muscles to contract while inducing a feeling of euphoria."

I didn't try to hide my open-mouthed gape.

"You gave them liquid orgasm?"

"Essentially. It'll keep them busy for days while we clean up their mess."

I shook my head.

"You're nastier than you look."

He smiled. "And you're softer than you look."

I turned away and examined the troll den. He was cozily packed away for a long sleep.

Mason squeezed my arm. "Before I cast the containment spell, help me cover him with bramble. That way the camouflage will be part of the spell."

I nodded.

We filled the empty cavities in the den with wet sand and pebbles. I scrounged for dead wood and handed branches to Mason. He laid them across the hole in a basket weave. I watched him work. His shirt was still damp, yet he showed no signs of cold. His hair had dried in unruly curls. I suspected he despised those curls. He was lean, but hard muscled, the only brawn showing in the cut of his shoulders. He would hold his own in a fight, but his allure was more than that. Everything about him suggested dark power. He wore black from head to toe, hair, clothes, boots. Even the gaze that he leveled at me was black. Yet I didn't fear him. And that scared the pants off me.

And I still couldn't figure out his particular brand of magic.

"Tired, Miss Greene?" He grinned and tugged at a branch in my hand. I had become lost in my scrutiny and he knew it. "I can finish this part myself."

A rock claw shot up and grabbed Mason by the throat, lifting him off the ground. The brambles caught the troll, but it was only a temporary cage. He shook Mason like a wolf with a kill. Branches snapped and flew. A splinter pierced my thigh. I fell against the living stone mountain and looked up at Mason. His eyes were closed and his lips moved in prayer or in magic. I couldn't tell which, but he wouldn't have time to finish either before the troll crushed his windpipe.

I drew my sword and aimed for the soft spot under the troll's chin again. I swung with all my strength and Mason screamed. The sound tore at my spine and I deflected my sword at the last minute.

My gods, what had I almost done? One strike of my sword to kill. Two would release his spirit. I had already pierced the troll's thick hide once. It hadn't killed him, but Valkyrie magic was unpredictable with immortals. A second might kill him. Or it could send his malignant spirit soaring into the night, free from the shackles of his heavy body to murder, rape and torture anyone in his path.

Crap.

I couldn't risk it. Instead, I dropped the sword into the stream and searched my pockets for a weapon. Any weapon. Mason flailed in the stone grip. I flung the roll of duct tape and it bounced on the troll's head. My other hand found the flashlight. I jumped on his back and beat him with the metal torch. He swatted me like a fly and I fell hard, hit my head on the river bed and came up sputtering water, flashlight gone.

Scrounging for my next weapon, I lunged again. My fists pounded on his skull. He head-butted me. Stars exploded behind my eyes, but I hung on. He roared, opening his great maw. I shoved the bug fogger in his mouth. Massive jaws shut and the can wedged between his stone teeth. The troll shrieked his fury, but the can stuck. Mason was limp in his grasp. I fumbled in my pockets again, thinking of the tranquilizers, but my hand closed on the flare gun instead. Barely hanging onto the slippery stones, I shoved the gun in the gap between his teeth and fired, praying to my great-grandfather, Odin, to boost the mortal weapon with the wrath of the gods.

The gun flared and bucked in my grip, and for the first time, I saw the troll's eyes. Two slits in the rock cracked wide with astonishment. He let Mason drop. The fogger burst in a cloud of foul chemicals. I fell, gasping as the troll exploded. Stones rained down on me, but I was too weak to do more than cover my face.

When the dust settled, I heard only the shushing of the river. Mason had to be dead. I should be dead.

"Kyra, don't move." Fear edged his voice. "There's a lot of rock on top of you. I'm going to shift it."

I couldn't nod, couldn't speak. A tear leaked down my face. It would have to do.

Mason worked quickly. One by one, I felt the stones lifting off me. My lungs filled with much-needed air. Tiny fingers prodding at my bruised body told me that the satyrs had returned to help. Finally, Mason brushed off the remaining debris and eased me to a sitting position.

"You need an ambulance," he said, taking his widget from his pocket and dialing. I blacked out before hearing the call.

Later—seconds or minutes—Mason handed me a water bottle. My fingers hurt to grip it. Pain shot up my arm when I tried to raise it to my lips. He took the bottle and dribbled water into my mouth. My throat burned when I drank. It was good to be alive.

Mason covered the troll den with twigs and set the wards in place that would keep the beast asleep for at least another century or until someone with more curiosity than sense tried to break it. When his magic flared, it was a rough, sweet sound like the first crickets of spring. I knew that I would recognize his magic from now on, just as I would recognize the sound of his heartbeat.

And I also knew exactly what kind of being he was—impossible as it seemed.

"I have to go now." I opened my eyes and Mason leaned over me. His face was close enough that I could see what I hadn't before. Small lines creased his eyes. Some called these laugh lines, but I couldn't imagine this hard man laughing enough to leave marks.

Birds chirped tentatively in the branches above. Dawn was almost upon us.

"You were very brave back there," he said.

"Nothing a girl can't fix with a roll of duct tape and a can of fogger."

He smiled. A slight dimple creased his right cheek and I ached for him. Not ached for want of him. Ached because the smile seemed so foreign to his face, as if he might crack with its weight.

"I don't want to leave you like this." He rubbed the tension from his neck. "But I have to."

"I know."

"The ambulance is on its way. I gave them the exact coordinates."

I nodded and it hurt.

He leaned in. "Thank you." His lips brushed mine with the whisper. From the disappearing shadows came a boyish giggle. Mason snarled at them and the satyrs scattered. He turned his black eyes back to mine and deepened his kiss. I found strength enough to lift my hand and twine my fingers in his curls. A dark moan escaped from him, and he carefully lifted me off the cold, hard ground. For one electrifying moment, I was suspended in his powerful arms. His heart battered at my door.

An unbidden call, one that even I couldn't hear, stopped him.

"The sun. I have to go." With gentle hands, he laid me back on the stones, pulled a blanket from his pack and covered me.

Everything hurt. The pains were too many to catalog. I'd broken some ribs. The rest of me was covered in cuts and bruises. Tears burned my puffy eyes, and I suddenly realized how alone I was in the world.

"Stay." I rasped. "Please."

Mason glanced at the lightning sky, then back at my battered face and nodded. He sat on the damp ground and took my hand in his. We listened to the first birds of the morning. A few minutes later, I felt his hand slip from mine. I opened one painful eye to find a stone man sitting beside me.

Mason was a gargoyle.

A siren wailed in the distance, coming for me.

"Mason?" I opened my eyes to darkness.

"No, ma'am."

The room adjusted around me. Not true darkness, then. Only a shaded window and a foggy head masking daylight.

And not Mason, who would be—what? Stone for the hours until dusk? Dead? How did gargoyle magic work?

Even if my brain wasn't clouded by pain and drugs, I didn't have the information I needed. Once I was better, I would have to remedy that.

"Who are you?" My words were thick. My tongue felt dry and swollen.

The man in the chair beside my bed held a cup of water with a straw to my lips and I drank. It hurt. The smell hit me now. Hospital. I was recovering in a hospital from…

Images came back to me. A river. Rock troll. Satyrs. Mason. A kiss.

"My name is Dutch," the man said. "I turned my head and painful lights exploded in front of my eyes.

"Rest easy," he said.

"Who…"

"I work for Mr. Mason. I am his daytime eyes, you might say. He wanted to be sure that you were taken care of after your…encounter."

"How long?"

"You've been in hospital for two days."

Two days? I healed fast thanks to my Aesir blood. Never before had I been unconscious for two days. I should probably be dead.

Dutch shifted in the chair. "Now you're awake, I should get the doctor."

"Wait." I reached for him. My arm was connected to wires and a clamp on one finger sent pulses to a nearby machine. "Mason. Is he okay?"

Dutch smiled

"Gargoyles are hard to kill, ma'am. He's more worried about you. Do you have family to take care of you when you're released?"

"Yes." Gita, my roommate and live-in nanny, would enjoy fussing over me.

Dutch nodded. "Good. Mr. Mason says that should you need anything, you need only call."

So he wouldn't come. Well, what had I expected? I could call. No reason to leave it all up to him. But did I want to? Could I get involved with another immortal with all the baggage they came with? The centuries of guilt, angst and ennui that built up in their souls, begging for release?

"My sword." I tried to rise. Paramedics had brought me here, but I couldn't remember if they'd retrieved my sword.

"Your weapon is safe," Dutch said. "Mr. Mason had me retrieve it and deliver it to your home. Your roommate took possession of it."

Dutch was smooth. He didn't even pause over the fact that my roommate was a banshee.

"Thank you." I lay back in the bed, now recognizing the uneasy feeling in my blood. My sword was too far away. The separation grated on my magic.

But the effort to stay awake was too much. I was asleep before Dutch reached the door.

5

I studied the pile of rocks and sticks that sheltered the sleeping troll. Mason's staff was driven deep into the middle of the heap, anchoring his sleep spell. That was the only evidence left of the battle I still saw so clearly in my nightmares.

The question of the troll's awakening still bothered me. According to Mason, he'd been in a deep stasis for over forty years. Something had disturbed his sleep. Was that something a happenstance like a stray ley-line flare? Or did someone deliberately wake him? It could also be possible that Mason's original sleep spell had simply worn out. I wasn't sure how those things worked. I could ask him. It would be a good excuse to make that first call. But I couldn't quite bring myself to do it.

Two weeks since our epic battle, I still hadn't heard from the mysterious gargoyle. That silence spoke volumes about his feelings for me. Or I should say, his lack of feelings.

Standing under the bridge with the chill water surging around my ankles, I opened my keening to the magic of this place. The troll's signature was a fuzzy miasma to my right. The river had its own trilling magic, and beneath that ran a ley-line—a deep, throbbing vein of Terra's magic. The magic of the earth.

I felt a tug on the hem of my jeans and looked down. A floppy red face peered up at me. The little squid latched onto my jeans and pulled himself up to rest on my boot.

"Hey, fella. You don't look so good." His red had grayed and mottled. I picked him up, and he settled like pudding in my hand.

"I bet you're not getting enough to eat in this creek." He gazed at me, and in his huge dark eyes, I recognized intelligence. Finding a squid in a creek in Montreal definitely wasn't a normal thing, so I'd suspected he was a fae creature. But now, he'd reached out to me twice, asking for help. And there was no doubt, he'd saved my life by distracting the troll.

Valkyrie Pest Control just gained a new rescue.

"I've got a big aquarium at home. You'll have to share it with Tucker, my abaia eel, but he's good people." I ran a finger along the side of his head and he made that trilling weeeeee noise. I took it for confirmation.

Overhead, the drumbeat of tiny hooves reverberated across the bridge. Then came the boyish shrieks, one after another as my snares caught three naughty satyrs.

"I think I'll call you Hunter. Does that work for you?" One tiny tentacle wrapped around my wrist and squeezed. "Good. Let's go round up a herd of goats, shall we?"

I glanced one last time at the pile of rocks, then vowed to let my memories sleep along with the troll.

WHERE THERE ARE SATYRS

June 13, 2079

I had an eventful few days. Eventful and painful. I got into a brawl with a rock troll. Yes, you read that right. Not the smartest thing I've ever done. I'll write a post about that in a few days, when I can wrap my head around it. For now, I am recovering at home, after three days in the hospital. Gita is acting like a fussy nanny. Or maybe I'm just bored from lying in bed for a week. I want to get back to work, but doc says I have to stay put for another few days. So I thought I'd tell you about another encounter I had the same night as the rock troll.

Let's talk satyrs. Or call them *silenos*, or fauns. They're all variations of the half-man, half-goat myth. Well, they're not a myth. I was called into a local school that was having trouble with some raunchy goats, terrorizing the kids and defacing the property. Turned out to be satyrs, not goats.

Here's how my encounter compared to the satyr myths:

The creatures were half human (on top) and half goat (below the waist), but the ones I encountered were boyish, at least in appearance. Their exaggerated sexual nature meshed with the stories I've read. And they had a mischievous bent. But I wasn't prepared for their strength. I saw three small satyrs move a pile of stone that would have taken a backhoe to move. And they did it in under an hour. I felt positively weak next to them.

And of course, where there are satyrs trotting across a bridge at all hours, there just has to be a troll. More on him later.

Thankfully, the satyrs spend their energy mostly on pranks and rutting. I'm not sure they are even aware of how awesome their strength is.

I've heard tales of satyrs down in the Olympian Ward. Can anyone verify that? As always, I'd love to hear about your encounters with satyrs, silenos, or fauns. Post them in the comments below.

Comments (5)

I love me some hairy man-child! Get better soon!

deathbyroses (June 13, 2079)

We had a satyr infestation here (Olympian Ward) about three years ago. The Ward Council banished them to the Inbetween, but we still see them lurking within the city slums once in a while. You can't ever really get rid of satyrs.

Hermes498 (June 14, 2079)

> Maybe some of your banished crew came north to Montreal?
>
> *valkyrie367 (June 14, 2079)*

I'm so sorry to hear of your injuries! Rest up and feel better soon!

cchedgewitch (June 14, 2079)

Stop filling the void with your heretical stories. There is a special place in the fires of hell for your kind.

GodsDove333 (June 15, 2079)

Rock Troll Encounter

June 16, 2079

I promised a post about my encounter with the rock troll. To be honest, I've been putting it off because it really shook me up. I'm still recuperating at home, but all this lying around is making me antsy. And I've been having nightmares. Maybe writing about it will help. So here goes.

As I mentioned in a previous post, I answered a job at a local school to get rid of some satyrs. These mischievous critters were taunting a rock troll. I have it on good authority that the troll had been sleeping under a bridge behind the school for over forty years. What woke it? I'm not sure. Maybe a stray flux from a ley-line? Has someone been performing magic rites nearby? As soon as I'm well enough, I plan to investigate.

But the troll was awake and grumpy. The satyrs running across its bridge and teasing it didn't help. I showed up with a tranq gun and some snares, expecting an easy capture and release.

That didn't happen. My weapons had little effect on the troll. I have the bruises and broken ribs to prove it. Only with the help of some bystanders was I able to subdue the creature. I am glad to say it is now back in stasis, hopefully to stay.

Anyone else encountered a rock troll? I'm curious to see how common these creatures are.

Comments (6)

There is a story about one in our ward, more of an urban legend really. I can't say if it's true or not. But the story says that a rock troll terrorized the first settlers here after the war. Killed a dozen people before Donal Hennigan killed it

and used the stones from the troll's body as the cornerstone for the first town hall. That was over fifty years ago. I can't verify the story's authenticity.
BlackJack4856 (June 16, 2079)

> Wow. That is a great story. I guess I got off lightly.
> *Valkyrie367 (June 16, 2079)*

So how did you finally kill it? Inquiring minds want to know.
TrophyHunter666 (June 17, 2079)

> The only way to kill a rock troll is with dynamite. Lots of it.
> *InnocentUntilNot (June 18, 2079)*

> > A bit of napalm should do the trick.
> > *TriggerHappy42 (June 18, 2079)*

Okay guys, I'm shutting down the comments on this one. I'd hoped to have an intelligent conversation, but as usual, you just want to watch the world burn.
Valkyrie367 (June 18, 2079)

A LOST CEPHALOPOD

June 20, 2079

The saga of my rock troll and satyr encounter continues. I'm glad to update that the satyrs have been safely trapped and re-homed. They can no longer bother the impressionable teens at the middle school. You can read the posts about the satyrs and the troll in the Archives.

A local gargoyle helped to trap the troll and put it into stasis. But before that, I found a truly unique creature in the stream that runs under the troll bridge. It is a cephalopod of some sort. Odd, I know. How could it survive in fresh water? True, the waters of Lake St. Louis have been brackish since the Flood Wars ended, but I found this critter in a stream well inland.

Here's the kicker: when I looked into his eyes, I saw awareness and intelligence. This proved to be the case. The little squid was instrumental in subduing the troll. I'm not exaggerating to say I'd be dead without him.

Today, I went back to check on the sleeping troll and the squid-thing was still lurking around. He didn't look too healthy, so I brought him home for now. I hope to find a new home for him.

Anyone know what it is? What do they eat? Leave your ideas in the comments below.

Update: August 3, 2079

Thanks to everyone who made suggestions about the mystery squid. I'm going with pygmy kraken. I named him Hunter. I did find a nice new home for him. A local dentist has a fabulous aquarium set up in his waiting room. He was delighted to have Hunter as his new addition.

Unfortunately, Hunter had other ideas. It seems some of the stories in the comments about pygmy krakens escaping and terrorizing people are true. Though I think Hunter is looking more for a good laugh than a scream of terror. It seems the kraken can fit through just about any opening. Staff and customers at the clinic were surprised (insert here: terrified, horrified) to find him in various places around the office, including coffee cups, the drain in the bathroom sink, the toilet, the supply cupboard…well you get the idea.

The dentist (who has a new nervous tic) has returned Hunter to me. And yes, I have experienced the kraken's tricks. I woke up to a squid in the glass of water by my bed this morning. But what can I say? I'm a sucker for big brown eyes. I think I'll keep him.

COMMENTS (5)

Hi from le Couven de Morelle, near Marseille in France. Our harbor was overrun by these beasts. They got into the engine room of many ships and destroyed much property. You should eradicate this pest before they spread.
laflamemorelle (June 20, 2079)

> Thanks for the advice. But I have just the one. No infestation in sight.
> *Valkyrie367 (June 20, 2079)*
>
> —

This is a pygmy kraken. Fae creature class 3. But I would argue that they have more intelligence and should be placed in class 2.
DrC-Biread (June 22, 2079)

Pygmy kraken definitely.

Zoogirl723 (June 22, 2079)

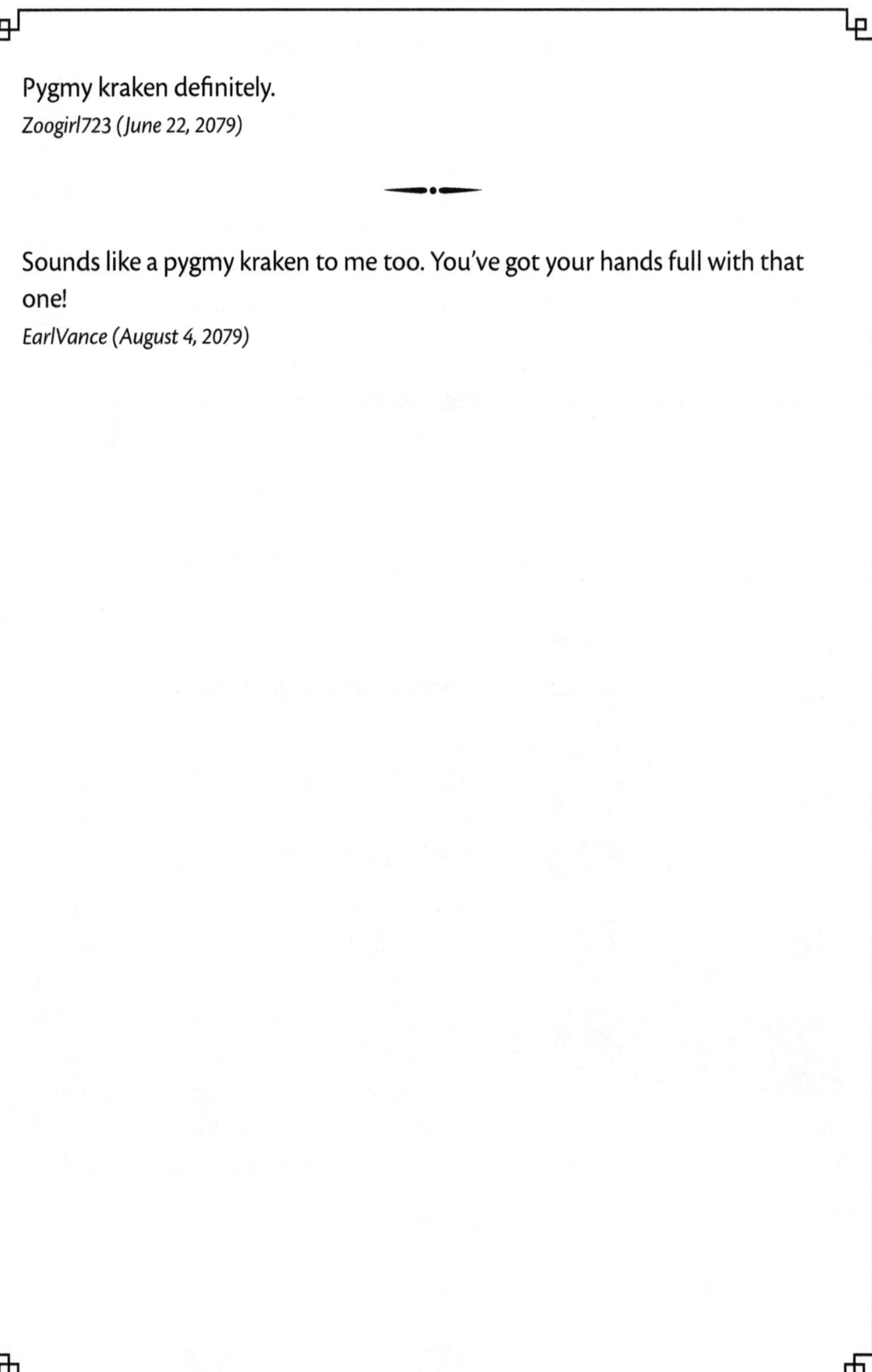

Sounds like a pygmy kraken to me too. You've got your hands full with that one!

EarlVance (August 4, 2079)

REVIEWS HELP EVERYONE

You probably know that authors love reviews, but do you know why? Reviews are important to every author, for the following reasons:

- They help other readers know what to expect from the book.
- They let me know how my books are received by readers.
- They help booksellers decide which books to show to new readers.

To leave your review for *Before Times, 3 Valkyrie Bestiary Prequels*, visit your favorite retailer or https://kimmcdougall.com/review-before-times

BOOK 5, *KELPIES DON'T FLY* IS NOW AVAILABLE!

Critter wrangler rule #13: Where there's one carnivorous horse, a herd will follow

For ten years, Kyra Greene thought she was the only Valkyrie this side of the rainbow bridge. Until she gets a stunning message from her cousin asking for bail money.

Facing the ghosts of her past isn't on Kyra's to-do list. All she wants is to settle into her new home with Mason and her menagerie of furred, feathered and scaled rescues. But her cousin's plea for help sets a new Inbetween adventure in motion. Kyra and her crew will find themselves on the wrong side of the law and going to war with a herd of murderous kelpies. But this time, Kyra might finally set past wrongs to right.

Find it at KimMcDougall.com/kelpies-dont-fly

Critter wrangler rule #2: When scary things run away, something scarier is coming.

A pest-controller with a soft heart can easily end up with an apartment full of rescues. When Kyra finds an abandoned baby dragon, she doesn't want to bring him home, but until she hunts down the brute trying to kill all the dragons and start a civil war among the fae, she's on babysitting duty.

Readers say Dragons Don't Eat Meat is "Very funny," "A sweeping adventure," "A slow burn romance." And more than one has said, "I want to be a supernatural pest controller too!"

Visit KimMcDougall.com/dragons-don-t-eat-meat to order your copy now, or continue reading for a preview.

DRAGONS DON'T EAT MEAT (PREVIEW)

CHAPTER

1

fter a long day of chasing pookas, moon-frogs and one particularly stealthy gremlin, all I wanted was a cup of tea and a hot bath. Not necessarily in that order. I sniffed myself. The bath would definitely come first. The gremlin had rolled in garbage to mask his scent. But he was Hub's problem now. That was the best part about taking commissions from the city. I was only responsible for trapping the nuisance critters, not re-homing them.

I pulled up to a storefront that had once been a mechanic's shop. A hand-painted sign over the office door proclaimed "Valkyrie Pest Control." The space was all mine and I was duly proud of it. I'd worked hard, building the business up from a part-time job I'd done mostly as favors to friends. I'd always had an affinity for animals. Bugs didn't faze me and when the fae came to town, it turned out they didn't daunt me either.

Too tired to unpack, I left my gear in the truck. A quick peek at the moon-frog caught on my last job showed the critter happily chewing the bars of his cage. About the size of a cantaloupe, he had bumpy, blue-green skin, big eyes and a wide mouth. Moon-frogs are voracious eaters with mildly acidic saliva. They can cause damage similar to termites, if termites were the size of rabbits. During most of the month, they're sluggish and easily caught. But when the full moon hits, the critter puffs up like a balloon covered in needle-sharp thorns that release a powerful hallucinogen. Nasty and dangerous but good for a quick high, they were hunted to near-extinction in the sixties. I hoped the cage would contain him for the night.

I was thankful my apartment took up the back half of my office. I wouldn't have to haul my aching bones far before I could peel off my jeans and drop into a hot bath.

The sun had long since set. The fickle street lamp on the corner of my parking lot flickered, throwing more shadows than light. I grabbed the moon-frog's cage and lugged it toward the office. A movement at the upstairs window told me that Mr. Murray was at his usual lookout.

"Hello, Mr. Nosy-pants." I waved to him and the curtain fell back into place.

Ryleah's car was parked beside the door. As the latest in a long string of assistants, I didn't have high hopes for Ryleah making it to the one-month mark. I wasn't a demanding boss, but the job could get a little hairy. And slimy. And bloody. My last assistant, Tiffany, fainted the first time I brought back a vampire slug. Who knew those things could move so fast?

After I bandaged her, Tiffany quit. Before her, John had been unable to deal with cleaning devil-rat blood off my tools. Before him…Well, there'd been other messes and other assistants who couldn't handle them. That Ryleah was still here, after eight o'clock on a Friday night, showed some gumption.

Inside, the office was dimly lit and silent. Two desks and a small sitting area filled the main room. Case files for past jobs were piled high on my desk. Cages, aquariums and terrariums lined two walls. Dozens of eyes peered from the gloom. My rescues were unusually subdued tonight. Even Clarence, my hyperactive basilisk, simply watched with wide eyes from his pen.

"Ryleah?" I dumped the moon-frog cage on my desk.

"Kyra! Shh! Over here." Ryleah peered from under her desk. "They're watching me!" Makeup was smeared under her eyes and a gob of green goo puckered her cheek. Gleeful chittering erupted from the shadows and two plump fur balls zoomed by, heading for the old garage-turned-gymnasium.

Ryleah squeaked, then choked back a sob.

I sighed.

"Alvin and Theo! I'm going to sell you as bait if you don't stop it right now!"

More chittering and a hunk of green cud landed on the floor by my feet. The madras knew I was bluffing. The mischievous rodents resembled guinea pigs and liked to chew hay into cud to throw at unsuspecting passersby. They had good aim too. I'd lost more than one assistant to their antics. And clearly, the new lock I'd spent a small fortune on did nothing to keep them in their cage. Little Houdinis.

"Come on." I helped Ryleah stand. "I'll catch them later. Any messages for me?"

She straightened her skirt and smoothed down her hair. I didn't mention the cud on her face.

"You've got no appointments this weekend, but Monday's turning out to be busy." She hiccuped as she flipped through a notepad. Her hands shook. "Three jobs in the morning, and…"

The bars of the moon-frog's cage gave way, and the fat critter plopped onto the desk. It jumped, landed on Ryleah's chest with a slimy splat, stared straight into her startled face and shrieked like its ass was on fire.

Ryleah shrieked right back.

I grabbed the frog before it could puff up and eject spiny thorns full of hallucinogenic venom right into her heart and dumped it into the wastepaper basket. Ryleah fell back, knocking over a chair while she clawed at the slime oozing into her cleavage.

"I'm…I'm…d-d-done." Her eyes blazed fiercely, but her chest heaved with the beginnings of hyperventilation. "N-n-no more." She grabbed her purse and ran out. I heard her car door slam and the engine flare to life. Tires skidded as she tore out of the parking lot.

"You can pick up your last check next week," I called weakly, knowing there was no way she'd ever be back. I'd mail the check.

I righted the chair and sat. Exhaustion deflated me. I would need to hire another assistant. Where would I find time for interviews? But if I didn't make time, I'd be in a worse way. I couldn't manage the day-to-day office affairs and trap critters too. Business was booming. I should have been happy.

I gazed at the creatures in cages that lined my office. Fae beasts, otherworld rodents, lizards taken straight from mythology, birds, bugs, and some I had yet to classify. Each critter in my care was orphaned or injured and could no longer survive alone. We had a symbiotic relationship. I cared for them and they filled my need for family.

The madras returned to twine around my ankles.

"This is all your fault." I picked up Alvin. His round butt settled in the palm of my hand. I stroked his silky brindled fur and he leaned into my touch. His face was rounded like a guinea pig's, but his lip split to show two prominent front teeth. Intelligent eyes watched me with affection. I had no idea what world he came from, but if the ley-net caught on, madras would be the next go-to pets.

"You scared poor Ryleah. I'll be lucky if I don't get sued for mental trauma again."

Alvin head-butted my chin. He knew I couldn't stay mad. I put him down and carefully transferred the moon-frog to another cage. No way I could wait until tomorrow to release him. I'd have to go tonight. I turned to unlock the door leading from the office to my apartment.

"Gita! I've got to go out again," I called into the dark apartment. Muffled sobbing answered from the coat closet. I knocked on the door. "Gita, did you hear me?"

The door opened and the scent of ocean brine hit me. A gray face with red-rimmed eyes peered out. Green-brown hair hung like swamp moss to her waist. Though technically another rescue, Gita was the closest thing I had to a live-in nanny and housekeeper. Banshees didn't make the best roommates, but I needed help with my charges, and I'd grown used to her crying.

"You should change yer shirt." She sniffled and tucked a lock of gray hair behind a gray ear. "You smell like shite."

"Thanks. Can you feed the horde?"

Gita nodded, wiped her nose on a soggy handkerchief and slammed the closet door. The wailing escalated until Mr. Murray banged on his floor with a broom.

"Sorry, Mr. Murray," I said. "We'll try to keep it down." Gita must have heard him too because her cries quieted to hiccupy sobs.

I grabbed a glass from the cupboard in the kitchen, found Hunter, my pygmy kraken nestled inside it and dumped him back in the aquarium, then rinsed the glass and gulped down as much water as I could hold. That would have to fill my stomach until I got home.

In the bedroom, I pulled off my shirt and picked another from the questionable pile of clothes on a chair. On a whim, I pulled out the braids that kept my hair out of the way while I worked and yanked a brush through my hair. Then I dabbed on lipstick.

I was no good at fooling myself, and I didn't even try to pretend the lipstick was for the moon-frog.

I was headed to Dorion Park. My trek would take me right by the home of Henry Mason, alchemist, Guardian and gargoyle. I'd last seen Mason over a year ago. We spent some quality time bleeding on each other after fighting a rock troll and shared one toe-curling, night-sweat-inducing kiss.

In the months since, he hadn't called. Typical. He'd left me hanging. Now, if I did see him—even if I found him in battle with a hell spawn—I wouldn't deign to throw a dagger his way.

But a little lipstick never hurt.

The preview has to end, but the fun goes on in Dragons Don't Eat Meat. Grab your copy now at:

https://kimmcdougall.com/dragons-don-t-eat-meat

About the Author

If Kim McDougall could have one magical superpower, it would be to talk to animals. Or maybe to shift into animal form. Definitely, fantastical critters and magic often feature in her stories. So until she can change into a griffin and fly away, she writes dark paranormal action and romance tales, from her home in Central Ontario. Visit Kim online at www.KimMcDougall.com

Want to find out more about Kyra's world?

Join Kim McDougall's reader group or learn more about the Valkyrie Bestiary series, including deleted scenes and more series fun at KimMcDougall.com

Poke around at Kyra's blog at ValkyrieBestiary.com

Other places you can follow Kim McDougall Books: Amazon, BookBub, Goodreads, Facebook, Twitter, or Instagram.

www.ingramcontent.com/pod-product-compliance
Lightning Source LLC
Chambersburg PA
CBHW051225210726
48290CB00003B/805